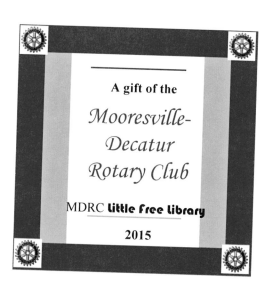

A gift of the

*Mooresville-
Decatur
Rotary Club*

MDRC **Little Free Library**

2015

Singled Out

a novel

Sara Griffiths

bancroft
press

Published by Bancroft Press "Books that enlighten"
P.O. Box 65360, Baltimore, MD 21209
800-637-7377
410-764-1967 (fax)
www.bancroftpress.com

Cover illustration, design, and interior design:
Tracy Copes; Daft Generation
tracy@daftgeneration.com

ISBN 1890862959/978-1-890862-95-4 (cloth) $19.95
ISBN 1890862967/978-1-890862-96-1 (pb) $14.95
Printed in the United States of America

First Edition

1 3 5 7 9 10 8 6 4 2

To Marielle

Chapter 1

I couldn't sleep. I kept staring at the red numbers on my bedside clock as if they would lull the tension out of me, but they only made me more anxious. Tomorrow would be the big day.

Earlier that afternoon, I'd been fumbling around my room trying to pack, asking my dad for the hundredth time if he still thought all of this was a good idea.

"Honey, we talked about this," he said. "You can't say no to this chance. I mean, if you honestly want to go to college, attending Hazelton will get you noticed."

And by "noticed," he meant on the field—the baseball field. I had a reputation in town as the only girl who could strike out the boys, and that's why the Hazelton School had offered me a scholarship. Weird thing was, my grades were less than great—in fact, they downright sucked. "I still can't believe they're letting me in with such a low grade-point average," I said.

"You heard what the athletic director said. It's not a big concern," my dad had said. "They want you to play ball. You should be grateful for the chance."

And he was right. I wasn't great at school, either socially or with grades, which, right now, were maybe good enough to get me into community college. I'd always hoped to get a baseball scholarship to college, but my grades were so crappy, scouts stopped coming to see me pitch. But if I could do well at Hazelton, on the field and in the classroom, maybe some college would take a chance on me.

I'd spent the past few months bored out of my skull, playing in the local summer league. I'd decided to pitch only because my high school coach suggested that playing in the over-sixteen league would give me more experience against better players. Unfortunately, he was wrong. The summer coach hardly ever played me. He only let me close out games, so I spent most of my summer perfecting the art of eating sunflower seeds and spitting them into a paper cup.

After junior year, I'd told my school coach that I was quitting baseball. It wasn't that I didn't like the sport anymore. In fact, up until last spring, I used to get so excited about baseball—it was the one thing I could do well. It had just become too easy, too predictable. I'd gotten too good. When I was a freshman and a sophomore, guys could hit me, but by junior year, I was a beast—no one could get a hit.

So when Mr. Sabatini first came to one of my summer games, I figured he was just another one of my high school coach's buddies there to persuade me to play my senior year.

But he wasn't. He was the athletic director at the most prestigious school in the state, the Hazelton School for Boys.

And he'd offered me a scholarship for my senior year.

At first, I thought his offer was crazy. I worried about being in a school full of guys. *Will they accept me?* I thought. The athletic director wanted me to try out for the baseball team, but would I even make it? The Hazelton School had a reputation for having one of the top teams in the state. But after talking to my dad, I realized accepting the scholarship was the right decision.

I really respected Dad's opinion on things. Without a mom around, he was my mom, and dad, and friend—kind of my everything. I trusted him. If he thought I should be happy about getting this chance, I figured he was probably right.

"I'll have to try out, though," I'd said nervously.

"And not flunk out, dummy," said my younger brother Dan, poking his head into my room.

I grabbed a pillow from my bed and flung it at Dan's head. Dan was fourteen and probably weighed all of a hundred pounds soaking wet. He was like a pole with a head. I loved him, but our love often took the form of sarcasm and the occasional headlock. My older brother, Brian, was all the way in Arizona, too far away to wrestle or mock me.

"You want to go outside so I can strike you out for the zillionth time?" I said to Dan.

"Hmm, I think you should hit the books instead, T."

"Ha ha," I said. "Dork."

"Dan," Dad said, blocking my next pillow throw, "don't you have a lawn to mow?"

He smiled. "Oh yeah. Twenty bucks is still the deal, right?"

"Yes, if it's done sometime before Christmas."

"No problem. Your money will soon be mine. Good luck with this mess, T. Don't forget to write," he said, pretending to cry as he scooted out of the room.

"He really is going to miss you, Taylor. He's just too much of a horse's butt to admit it," my dad said, stepping over the clothes piles forming on my bedroom floor. "And despite what he says, we all know you're not stupid."

I knew I was no genius, but I had never really cared. School was always just something I had to do, like a household chore.

"Jury's still out on that one," I said.

"You've spent the last few years focusing all your attention on baseball—well, baseball and Justin," Dad said.

Justin was my ex-boyfriend, and forever my friend. A couple years back, we dated for a while, but once he left for college, we kind of went into the friend zone, which was fine with me, because we were always better as friends than as anything else. Now he'd be spending the year in Spain. I already missed him.

"Maybe this'll be a great opportunity to try the academic thing for a while," Dad said. "You know, I don't love you only because you play ball. I should have pushed the academic thing more."

"Hey," I said, "baseball is what brought us back together."

He nodded. "But for a time, it was also what kept us apart."

Years ago, when my dad and I barely spoke, I was sure he hated me because he was embarrassed to have a daughter who played baseball better than the boys, and especially his sons. I quit playing when I was ten, even though I loved the game, because I thought that's what he wanted. It took a lot of counseling and talking for both of us to realize it wasn't my baseball playing that had distanced us. We were both trying to cope with the fact that my mother, without any real explanation, had left us.

"I guess that's one of the things that make it so hard to leave," I said. "I was without you for a long time." I was trying not to get choked up. "What if that happens again?"

He sat down on my bed. "Taylor, no matter where you go or what you do, I'm just a phone call away. And I promise you: We will never let something come between us again. Okay?"

At times like these, when big changes were happening in my life, I felt my mother's absence the most. My dad was affected by that void, too. I didn't ask him about her anymore. It made him really sad when I did. Besides, if she really wanted to talk to me, she knew where to find me.

Sometimes, I wondered if she regretted leaving us which, to me, was the height of selfishness. I occasionally thought about looking for her, but I didn't want to hurt my dad and, honestly, if she didn't want to see me, I didn't think I could handle the rejection. I'd just stick with one parent for now.

I gave Dad a big hug and let out a few tears. He stood up and grabbed a suitcase, which was now fully packed. "Should I bring this one down?" he asked.

I nodded and rubbed my eyes. "Yeah, go ahead. What the hell?"

"Language, please," he said as he pulled the suitcase down the hall to the top of the stairs.

"Sorry," I said, cracking a smile.

"Yeah, that's what I get, raising a daughter who plays ball. You've got a trucker's mouth. Bet they don't tolerate that at Hazelton."

"I'll wash it out with soap before we leave tomorrow."

He smiled and carried the bag down the stairs. I took a deep breath and cracked my knuckles.

I spent the next few hours trying to pack the rest of my stuff. The good thing was that the school was only fifty miles or so from our home in New Jersey, so if I found myself crying for my daddy after a few days, he was only a short car ride away.

At least I wouldn't be the only girl at Hazelton. There were two others coming. One of the girls, Gabby, was also an athlete, and also from Jersey—a varsity basketball player. She was also a senior, but I didn't know much else about her. The second girl was there strictly for academics. I think she was some sort of math whiz.

We'd be the first three girls ever to attend Hazelton.

I ended up filling only one other suitcase. I didn't have much of a wardrobe. Anyway, from what I'd read, I'd have to wear a uniform to class. I panicked when I pictured myself in a plaid skirt, but the school promised I'd have a few choices, including pants. There's nothing goofier-looking than putting a dress on a girl who usually wore sweats. In any event, it probably wasn't in the school's best interest to have girls in skirts running around a school full of boys.

Now I lay in bed, wide awake. I gave up trying to sleep and, eventually, my room started to fill with light. I heard cars moving down the street, and my neighbor letting his dog out, and I knew it was almost time to go.

After a quick breakfast that I hardly touched, I walked back upstairs. Dan was still asleep, and I didn't want to wake him so early, so I just peeked in and whispered goodbye.

Damn, I was nervous.

Chapter 2

At Hazelton, I was not going to live in the normal dorms with the other boys. Instead, I was assigned to live with Dr. Richards, the assistant headmaster, and his wife and young son, who were the main occupants of one of the largest houses on campus. The headmaster, Dr. Colton, had told my dad that the Richards house had twenty-four rooms and, in a pinch, could easily serve as a dorm.

"Mr. Dresden, good to meet you," Dr. Richards said as he shook my dad's hand. "And this must be Taylor," he added, turning and extending a hand to me as well. "The students around here all call me Dr. Rich."

Dr. Rich was well over six feet tall and had really broad shoulders. I was a bit intimidated by him, but he seemed friendly enough. Inviting us into a huge living room, he continued, "Curfew is 8:30 on school nights and 10 on weekends."

"You don't waste any time getting to the nitty gritty, huh?" Dad said.

"Student safety is vital to us at Hazelton, and learning begins at home. This will be Taylor's home for the next school year. As assistant headmaster, I believe a child cannot learn if he or she doesn't feel safe."

I don't know why they used words like "headmaster." To me, it seemed like everyone was being snooty for the sake of being snooty.

Mrs. Richards showed me to my room and gave me a tour of the house while my dad talked with Dr. Rich in the den. Mrs. Richards seemed really sweet. She held her son, Matthew, who she told me had just turned two. He was giggling to himself as she showed me the house.

The place was a mansion, and it was filled with spacious hallways and vaulted ceilings. The third floor was reserved for just the Richards family, and the second floor was for students.

"We have, on occasion, had some of the boys stay here when the dorms were overcrowded, or when there were problems, but this is the first time we've ever had girls. I apologize if the room décor is a bit masculine," Mrs. Richards said as we climbed the wide staircase. "Since you are the first girl to arrive, you get first choice."

I followed Mrs. Richards as she walked down the long second-floor hallway. I had never seen a hallway with a window at the end of it, and through it, you could see the entire huge, beautiful campus. And although this giant place was daunting, I felt smarter just staring out the window. "Taylor?" Mrs. Richards said as she stood by a nearby door.

"Oh, sorry," I said, following her toward the room.

"Here's your first choice." She opened the fourth door on the right. "What do you think?"

All dark wood with blue curtains, the room contained old wooden furniture and, in a far corner alcove under a small window, was tucked an overstuffed leather chair. The walls were adorned with paintings of different sports. Over the bed was a picture of a crew team rowing under a bridge. There was a big paddle over the desk that said "Hazelton 1953." And there were baseball caps with H's, obviously for Hazelton, tacked over the closet. On the desk in the opposite corner sat a new laptop.

"See what I mean about it being rather boyish?"

I wasn't sure why, but I immediately fell in love with the room. It was just the kind of room I thought only smart, over-privileged kids going to Princeton would get to sleep in, and I was thrilled at the thought of it being mine, at least for a while.

"Come on, I'll show you the other rooms."

I didn't move. "No, I think I'll take this one."

She was shocked. "You sure?"

I smiled. "Yeah, I like this one. Is that computer mine?"

"Yes, the headmaster had it sent over this morning." Matthew started to fuss and attempted to wiggle out of her arms. "All right, Mattie, just a minute," she said to him. "Well, Taylor, since you like the room, I'll have Dr. Richards bring up your things." She left me alone to settle in.

I walked around the room for a minute. I ran my hand along the wooden desk and walked over and peeked out the window. If school sucked, at least I could hide out here all marking period, or quarter, or whatever these fancy people called it.

I looked at the old Hazelton baseball hats. I wondered if it was acceptable to wear them, then decided I'd first have to feel these people out. After a few minutes, I went downstairs to see if the discussion between Dr. Richards and my dad was over.

When I entered the den, Dad was getting up off the couch.

"All right then, Mr. Dresden, if you have any questions, do not hesitate to call any time. This is Taylor's home now, so no office hours apply if you need to reach us."

"Good to know. She's also got her cell phone if she needs me," Dad said.

"Okay, well, I'll give you two a few minutes to say your goodbyes." He shook my dad's hand again and headed back toward the foyer.

"Come on, walk me to my car," Dad said, throwing an arm around my shoulder. We walked slowly out the front door.

At the car, Dad placed the papers Dr. Rich had given him onto the backseat, and then stood next to me. "You take care, kiddo, okay?"

I bit my bottom lip as I felt a fresh wave of fear wash over me.

He leaned in and gave me a big bear hug. "You'll be fine."

I pulled back and nodded, trying to be strong.

"I'm just an hour away," he said, opening the car door and settling in behind the wheel. He had tears in his eyes, too. He put the car in drive. "I love you, sweetie."

"Love you, too, Dad."

"Don't let those rich boys give you any crap," he said, resting his elbow on the car window.

"Language," I said, dragging out the word the same way he always did.

As the car lurched forward and disappeared, I took a deep breath and headed back inside. This would not be easy.

Chapter 3

I spent the next hour unpacking some of my stuff. I still didn't feel comfortable putting everything into the dresser, so I left one suitcase packed and put it on the floor of the closet.

All of a sudden, there were voices in the hall. My door was ajar, and I heard Mrs. Richards coming up the staircase, talking to another girl. I figured it had to be Gabby. Mrs. Richards had told me the girl genius wouldn't be living on campus. She was only a sophomore, and her parents didn't want her away from home at such a young age.

"And this is your floor," I heard Mrs. Richards say. "Let me introduce you to Taylor."

She knocked on the door. "Taylor?"

"Yeah, come on in," I said.

Standing in the doorway was Gabby Foster. She was black, easily six foot two, and probably weighed all of 120 pounds. Her hair was long and straight, and both her ears were double-pierced. She was dressed in a pair of boy's gym shorts and a tank top that would have showed the slightest bit of belly, except that hers was flat and rock-hard. "Taylor Dresden, Gabby Foster," said Mrs. Richards.

Gabby reached out for my hand. "Hey, Taylor, nice to meet you," she said confidently.

"Yeah, you too."

"You're the pitcher, right?"

"Yep."

"Yeah, I read about you in the paper a couple times."

She had? Maybe she was just saying that to be nice. Of course, I had done a lot of interviews before school had ended in June. "Uh, thanks," I said. I didn't know what else to say. I had never heard of her, so I just stood there and let an awkward silence happen. *Damn, I wish I were better at this social crap.*

Gabby turned to Mrs. Richards. "So, me and Taylor sharing, or what?"

"Oh, no, let me show you what we have to choose from."

"Cool. Taylor, peace," she said, pointing in my direction as she left the room.

Gabby seemed like the type of girl who had lots of friends, and so she probably thought I was an anti-social weirdo, which I suppose I kind of was. I'd have to brush up on basketball. At least then, I would have something to talk about with her.

Later that morning, our school uniforms were delivered to our rooms. I heard Gabby, who had ended up next-door, groan through the walls. "I don't even think a supermodel could look good in this stuff!" she said.

There was a selection of white shirts: two short-sleeve polos, two long-sleeve button-downs. There was also a pullover v-neck sweater and a cardigan, all with a navy blue "H" emblem trimmed in gold. There were a few pairs of pants in navy blue and two skirts. I was no slave to fashion, but even I thought I'd look like a guy in these outfits. During recent school years, I'd been a jeans-and-fitted-t-shirt kind of girl. In the summer, I wore tank tops and board shorts.

Before long, Gabby reappeared in the doorway. "Hey,

Taylor, you think this is acceptable?" She wore the new school skirt with her tank top, the cardigan tied around her waist like a belt. She actually looked decent.

"I think that works," I said, laughing. "I'm sure the boys would approve."

She looked at herself in the mirror hanging on the back of my closet door. "Oh please, I have a boyfriend," she said. "Not that I'm married, but I don't think these guys would know what to do with a black girl."

I wasn't exactly sure if what she said was supposed to be funny. I gave it a half-laugh. I was afraid of the uncomfortable silence coming again. *Ask her about something, anything,* I thought. *Her boyfriend.* "How long you guys been together?"

She shut the door. "Oh, let's see, I think it's been about eight months."

"That's pretty serious."

"I guess. He promised to pick me up every Friday after school, which should keep him honest."

It sounded as if I'd be the only girl here alone on the weekends. "So how come you decided to come to Hazelton?" I asked her.

"Two words: college scholarship. You?"

"Pretty much the same."

"My parents made me come here," she said, stepping away from the mirror.

"Ditto."

"Hmm," she said. "Well, I got to go make my room livable. Can you believe all this old-fashioned stuff? It's like a museum in here."

"I kind of like it," I said, feeling a bit embarrassed.

"Oh, you're out of your mind," she said with a laugh.

I shrugged. "I just like things simple."

She walked out into the hall. "Well, give me 'til tomorrow, and you can come check out my room. Bet you'll change your mind."

"Have fun," I said.

Later that afternoon, we had to go to the class orientation meeting. We basically sat in a big auditorium and listened to different teachers and other important people give speeches about how important learning was and how great Hazleton was. Gabby and I sat together in the back so we wouldn't get too many stares. We figured the boys could have their chance to ogle us tomorrow, on the first day of classes.

I was happy to be stuck in the boring lecture, though. It was so weird being here, and I didn't know what I was supposed to be doing. I hoped the next few days would be just as structured and busy, so I wouldn't think about the fact that I was away from home and missing my dad and house, and even my goofy brother.

Following the lecture was a tour of the campus for new students. Most were freshmen, except for the three *amigas*: me, the basketball star, and Tara Kwan, the brain. Kwan was petite and quiet. When I said hello to her, all she did was sort of nod and look down at the ground.

Then we were quickly huddled together for a picture—the local paper was there to document the first female students ever to attend Hazleton. The three of us had to stand out on the steps together. I was amazed that the newspaper had nothing more interesting to write about. Maybe it was bigger news than I thought to have girls here.

After years of playing on an all-boys team, I was strangely used to nosy newspaper reporters. One asked us a few quick questions, mostly about where we were from and if we liked the school so far. Another reporter asked Gabby what she thought of the Abernathy incident.

"Who's Abernathy?" Gabby asked. "Is he a basketball player?"

After hearing the exchange, the headmaster told the reporters that the Q&A was over, then escorted us into the building. "Sorry about the annoying questions, ladies," Dr. Colton said as he closed the door behind us. He seemed a bit flustered by the reporters and I wondered why, but I didn't ask because I was looking forward to seeing the rest of the campus.

About sixty freshman boys in golf shirts followed the tour guides, while we three *amigas* pulled up the rear. The gym annex was our first stop, and Gabby's eyes lit up when she saw the court. "I have died and gone to heaven," she said, loudly enough to turn most of the heads of the freshmen.

"It is nice," I said, which got the heads to turn again. The floor was so shiny with lacquer I could almost see myself in it. Instead of bench bleachers, there were real seats on both sides. The electronic scoreboard looked like something the Knicks would have, and the ceiling had to be twice as high as that of a normal gym. "One problem with this joint, though," I said to Gabby.

"What?"

"No girls' locker room," I said, pointing to the "Men" sign.

"I'll just get changed with them," she joked. "No problem there."

The rest of the campus was just as perfect. The Hazelton baseball stadium was gorgeous. It was like a miniature version of a big-league stadium—seats that wrapped around the entire field, an electronic scoreboard, and real dugouts below the playing field. I couldn't wait for spring.

After the tour, Gabby and I sat on one of the benches in the courtyard. "Hey, Gabby?" I said.

"Yeah?"

"What kind of grades you get back at your old high school?"

"Eh, not great. Mostly B's, some C's."

"Sounds better than me."

"Why do you want to know?"

"Just wondering," I said. As we walked down all the clean, wide hallways, I began to wonder whether doubt that I belonged in such a beautiful place. I wasn't smart enough, and there were plenty of girls out there who had busted their butts in school and deserved this opportunity far more. What was I good at? All I could do was throw a baseball.

"There are plenty of athletic girls out there who have good grades," I said. "So why us?"

"I think we're the only ones who have experience playing against boys."

I nodded. "I guess. But why not just give academic scholarships? Why'd they want us on their sports teams?"

"Never thought about it," Gabby said. "I heard it was to honor some woman who was a big shot at the school and died or something. Maybe it was her dying wish or something."

I laughed. "I find it hard to believe any woman from around here cared about me throwing curve balls."

"True. Well, maybe it has something to do with making money," she said. "That's usually what all these stuffy people care about."

Chapter 4

Classes began the next day at 7:45. I put on the white polo shirt and navy blue pants, because there wasn't much else to choose from. I certainly wasn't going to wear the skirt.

In order to not look like a total boy, I added the string choker necklace that Justin had given me before he went away to college. The brown string had a little circular medallion with a grizzly bear's face etched on it. He said it was for strength, and sometimes I wore it underneath my uniform when I thought I was going to have a tough day on the mound. Strangely enough, I hadn't put it on in over a year. Today, I thought I might need it.

Gabby was already downstairs in the kitchen. She had chosen the same outfit, but she looked a lot more like a girl than I did. She had put on big hoop earrings and shiny lip gloss. Some people have style, and some, like me, don't have a clue. Gabby was finishing a bowl of cereal, but I was too nervous to eat.

"You ready?" I said to her.

"Let's do it." She pushed her chair back and we made our way toward the front door. I appreciated how quickly Gabby had sort of adopted me as her friend.

We walked across the campus toward the main building.

"Look," Gabby said, pointing to the steps. There were two TV camerapeople filming our entrance and a reporter standing nearby with a microphone.

"Geez, they really are desperate for a story around here." I tried not to look at the cameras, but Gabby waved and winked.

I wished I was that bold.

Unfortunately, Gabby and I did not have any classes together. Gabby figured they wanted to spread out the girls, make it look to the press like there were more of us.

Classes at Hazelton were small, usually only about twelve students. It was not unusual to find juniors and seniors in the same classes, with even some extra-smart sophomores here and there.

My first class of the day was Trigonometry. I never understood why they didn't just call it fancy math. No matter what it was called, I would be lucky to pull a C in Trig. I had the sinking feeling that the work here would be even harder than at my old high school.

Since it was the first day of school for everyone, the teacher, Mr. Moesch, assigned seats. The desks were in rows, and I was so happy when I was directed to the back chair by the window. The boy to my left smiled, raising his hand in a friendly wave. His light brown hair was in a bowl cut that just about covered his eyes. I nodded hello back at him.

"I'm Ben," he whispered.

"Taylor," I replied.

"Yeah," he said, nodding, "we know."

I gave him a nervous half-smile.

Mr. Moesch immediately started his lecture, and I struggled to take notes fast enough. My hand began to cramp after twenty minutes, and I took to picking at my hangnails. I had no idea what he was talking about anyway.

When the bell rang, I was abruptly brought back to reality. As I inched toward the door, I fumbled through my bag, looking for my schedule. Mr. Moesch smiled and said, "Welcome, young lady." Ugh, I hated that term—"young lady." I forced a smile and headed out.

Ben was sort of hanging back in the hall. It appeared he was waiting for me. With the way everyone was staring at me, but trying to act as if they weren't, I felt like a circus freak. I wished I were on the mound pitching. It would be so much easier to face all these preppy guys with a ball and a glove in my hand. I could take them all down.

I thought back to the advice of my old guidance counselor: When you're nervous, just imagine the batter's behind in the count, with no balls and two strikes. You have the advantage.

But before I reached the Ben guy, he was suddenly pulled aside and into the men's room by a taller, more attractive look-alike. I wondered if the guy was his brother, or if the resemblance was just my imagination. All the guys sort of looked the same around here. Whoever the look-alike was, he looked pissed. I hung back for a minute to see if Ben would return, but he didn't. I had the strange feeling this had something to do with me. *But how could it? I just got here. Oh well,* I thought as I looked down at my schedule and stared down the hall at the classroom numbers. *Time for Spanish.*

The morning dragged on, and by lunch, I felt overwhelmed and exhausted. The café at Hazelton—"cafeteria" wasn't snooty enough—looked far nicer than any school eating-place I had ever seen. It was more like a lounge. There were round tables, and even sofas and coffee tables to sit at. It was a lot less pressure for a new kid to sit at one of these than at the typical long cafeteria tables that forced you to make friends with whoever was there.

Here, I bought a sandwich and sank down into one of the couches. I didn't need friends anyway. Having gotten by with so few all these years, being alone was kind of comforting, like an old pair of slippers. It was a lot less pressure not having to impress anyone or make small talk. Still, I was happy to see Gabby finally appear in the café, and I waved her over.

She plopped her large shoulder bag next to me. "I'm going to grab a bite. Be right back. Want anything?"

"No, I'm good."

When she returned, she started talking. "Can you believe this place? I don't think I ever got so much homework on the first day of school, and I'm due in the gym for tryouts today, which I assume are just a formality, right?" she said in one breath before taking a big bite of her sandwich.

"I guess," I said. "I assume we both have to try out just in case we got really bad over the summer or something."

"Well, I played on a summer team, so I feel good to go. You do summer league down in Evansville?"

"Yeah. It sucked, though."

"What else do you do down in South Jersey?"

"Not much."

"You got a big family down there?"

"It's just me and my dad and my brother," I said.

"Where's your mom? Your parents divorced?" said Gabby.

"Sort of. My mom just bailed on us when I was five. Haven't seen her since." I didn't want to make Gabby uncomfortable with my broken home story, so I added, "But it's no big deal, really."

Gabby nodded, and was quiet for a minute. She took a sip of her soda before asking, "So, what class do you have next?"

After the day ended, I walked back to Dr. Rich's house. It felt strange sharing the place with his family. I figured I would wait a few weeks, and then ask if they could find me a private room in one of the dorms. Being in a house made me miss home more. Maybe the dorm would be more businesslike, and I wouldn't miss my dad and my brother so much.

Overall, my first day was boring and, aside from all the staring, uneventful. My book bag was certainly heavier than when I started, and I forced myself to go up to my room and organize my desk. Maybe I would even look at my Trig homework, but I didn't make myself any promises.

When Gabby returned from tryouts, she was wiped out. She tapped on my door to deliver the news.

"How was it?" I asked.

"It was tough, but the coach had good things to say. They post the list tomorrow. Practice starts the next day."

"Sounds like you're in," I said.

"Let's hope," she said. "I'm gonna hit the shower."

"K. See you down at dinner."

Gabby, it seemed, was well on her way to making the team, which boded well for me. I slept well that night in my new blue room.

Chapter 5

Things got weird the next day. After Gabby and I walked to the gym to see her name proudly posted on the basketball team's varsity list, we parted ways to head to our first-period classes, and I noticed that the boys who'd been staring at me the day before were intentionally avoiding eye contact today. It was as if I'd been labeled some disease they didn't want to catch.

The second day of school was also when I figured out which student was really in charge. I admit that when he first appeared, he struck me as something to see. I wasn't usually one to go ga-ga over a guy's looks, but the first time I saw him walking toward me in the hall, I felt as if I needed an extra breath of air. I soon realized he was the same guy who'd shoved Ben into the men's room yesterday, but yesterday I hadn't gotten such a good look at him.

He was at least six feet tall, and thin, with wide shoulders, like those of a swimmer. His face had a strong, defined bone structure, like a model's. He had dark brown eyes and hair that looked black from far away. It was cut short in the back, but hung down just enough in the front so he would feel the constant need to brush it out of his face.

I also couldn't help noticing his hands. That second day, I was reaching for the door to my chemistry class at the same time he was doing the same, and so we touched hands, ever so briefly. His hands looked as strong as a grown man's, but felt soft like a child's. He had barely beaten me to the knob, and he turned his shoulder into me as he opened the door and held it for the guys behind him, leaving me squashed between the door and the wall.

Since it was the first day of Chemistry, the teacher called roll. I paid close attention to who raised their hands when their names were called.

"Samuel Barrett?" the teacher called.

"Present," said the boy who had squished me against the door.

Throughout the lecture, it was obvious that all the other boys in the class looked to this Barrett guy before doing anything. I assumed he must serve some important role at Hazelton. He had to be a senior, too, because only seniors were in this class. He seemed pretty full of himself, and based on how often he answered the teacher's questions, he was obviously pretty smart as well.

From that second day on, I felt a coldness every time Samuel Barrett was near me—as if, without speaking, he was saying, "You're not welcome here." He never spoke a word to me, and he looked over my head whenever I passed him in the hall. And it seemed he had told everyone to treat me the same. I decided his behavior was not my fault. I chalked it up to him just being an over-privileged snob and a sexist pig. That was easier to deal with than thinking there was something wrong with me.

From listening in the halls and gossiping with Gabby, I found out that Sam had a reputation for being both a star student and a star athlete. Ben Barrett, the guy I met the first day of school, was, in fact, his fraternal twin.

One day, I noticed Samuel Barrett in the picture of last year's baseball team, which hung in the trophy case. Next to his name were the words "Team Captain." Sitting next to him was the brawny blonde guy from my English class, William Tuttle, who was listed as a pitcher. I guess I would have to deal with that when the season started.

Before I knew it, the first week was over and my first weekend away from home was upon me. During the week, it had been easy figuring out what to do, because school and sleeping had taken up most of my time. But I didn't really know what to do with my free time. When school was out, I was told, most of the students studied and hung with friends, but I avoided studying like the plague and I didn't know anyone yet.

Gabby seemed nice, but she spent most of her time locked up in her room, on her cell phone. She was all about her boyfriend Jordan back at home, and on Friday afternoon, she'd left to go home for the weekend.

I promised myself I would at least stick it out the first weekend. I wasn't homesick—just unsure what to do with myself. I had started taking long runs after dinner each night. The school campus was full of winding trails to explore. The school food was making me feel fat, too, and I had to stay in good shape during the fall and winter if I wanted to kick butt against rich preppy brats in the spring.

That first weekend was pretty lonely. Dr. and Mrs. Richards were actually quite nice, although they were difficult for me to relate to. Dr. Rich always sounded like a headmaster—at dinner, when playing with his son, and even when taking out the garbage. It was kind of strange. I tried to join them for dinner and ate my other meals at the school café. They went out on Saturday afternoon for a few hours. They asked me to join them, but I said no.

I called my dad to chat about my first week, checked out every room in the house—even those on the third floor, not out of nosiness but out of boredom—and then settled down on the couch. I sat in the huge sunken living room watching TV. I flipped through the channels, but the Richardses had only the basic cable package, so there wasn't much on. I stopped at a local channel when I heard the word Hazelton. There was a shot of Gabby and Kwan and me. Leaning forward on the couch, I turned up the volume.

". . . Abernathy's lawsuit against Hazelton was put on the back burner this week as Hazelton welcomed its first female students," said the reporter. "The girls attending Hazelton were awarded the Mary Francis Halpert scholarship, named for Mary Francis Halpert, the wife of one of the founding members of the school and a major advocate of women's rights. When Dr. Colton, school headmaster, was asked if the scholarship was simply a ploy to rebuild the school's reputation, he replied that the two circumstances were unrelated. Abernathy's lawyers are still trying to persuade some former Hazelton students to serve as witnesses on Abernathy's behalf. Still to come after the break, the local forecast with—" I shut the TV off.

Hmm. I wonder why this Abernathy person sued the school. I considered how I felt about possibly having been brought here just to make the school look better. For the moment, I decided I didn't really care. After all, they had let me in with my bad grades, so I supposed I kind of owed them one. They were making me look better than I actually was.

I glanced at the clock. It was almost 3 p.m. I had to get out and do something, if only to clear my head.

Because it was a sunny September afternoon, I figured I could walk downtown and find a place to buy an iced coffee to help end my persistent craving. The Richards family didn't keep any caffeinated drinks in the house. Maybe I'd carry back a few cans of cola contraband as well. I shoved some money into the back pocket of my jeans and grabbed a hoody. I walked down the long drive to the front gates, turned left, and followed the sidewalk downtown.

The town of Hazelton was only about a half-mile walk from school. The town was, in a word, quaint. There were bookshops, coffee shops, and antique stores. There were lots of locals strolling up and down the main street eating ice cream, window shopping, and pushing fancy strollers. The sidewalks were all red brick, and the shops all had different-colored shutters on the second floor windows that served as apartments for some of the local college kids. Hazelton College was just north of town. Mrs. Richards had told me it was a very popular school for drama and art.

As I walked among groups of people, a sudden fear of seeing someone from school came over me. Not that I knew anyone really, but it would be weird to see any of the boys I had passed in the hall all week out here in my street clothes. Suddenly, I wished I had on my school uniform instead of a tank top. The school uniform had become a bit of a security blanket for me, and here, without it, I felt kind of exposed.

But before I could finish obsessing about my choice of outfit, my fear became a reality. The Barrett boys were coming out of one of the shops a few stores ahead of me. *Crap. If I turn around, it will be too obvious.* I made a quick decision to just say "hi" to the Ben guy if he made eye contact, since he had introduced himself to me on day one—although he'd chosen not to speak to me since. If Sam the snob had an issue with me, that was his problem.

Ben and Sam spotted me at the same time.

"Hi," I said, and then kept on walking at the same pace. As I expected, I was ignored. I didn't let it bother me, though. What did I care? I was on an iced coffee mission. Screw them.

Soon enough, I saw my refuge—Café News. The sign read, "Coffee, Tea, and Treats." My spirits were quickly lifted. I went in and fell in love with the place.

It was almost as cozy as my room. There was a coffee bar along one wall, and tons of comfortable chairs and couches scattered about. Some students played chess at the tables. Others sat alone, lost in their laptops. I ordered a large iced coffee with a lot of milk and sugar. I wanted to sit, but I didn't have a book or computer to hide behind, so I took the coffee to go.

I walked up and down the town's streets, peering in the windows and enjoying my iced coffee. It was so much better than the coffee from the convenience store back home. I went into a drug store and bought a few more notebooks for class, because as the first week in classes had shown me, I was going to go through a lot of paper taking notes.

As I was paying, I heard whispering behind me. I turned, trying not to make it obvious, and saw a few boys I recognized from Hazelton. They made some obscene gestures with their tongues, and I made a quick exit out the door.

Jerks!

Chapter 6

After surviving my first lonely weekend, I was kind of looking forward to school on Monday, because I was supposed to meet with the athletic director about off-season training. Hazelton had a great gym. I knew that. But they also had, I was told, special instructors to work with during the winter to get me prepared for baseball season. Practice didn't start until late February. I was excited about having a trainer to keep me in shape in the winter months. At my old high school, I hadn't done much in the fall and winter other than run and use some of the machines at the school gym, which were more dangerous than effective because they were so old.

After another quiet school day of being ignored and acquiring piles of notes and homework, I walked down to the gym offices for my meeting. Gabby had not only met with everyone, but had already started practicing with the team. To hear her on the subject, it sounded like basketball practice was going really well. I hoped that if she had an easy transition with her team, I would with mine.

I reached the office door and tapped lightly on the glass.

"Come in!" I heard a man yell.

When I entered, there were three men sitting around the office. Two were on metal folding chairs, and the one I recognized from the summer, Mr. Sabatini, the athletic director, was sitting on the desk. They were all looking up at the TV that hung in the far corner. I looked up at it, too, and was surprised to see it was me on the screen.

"Miss Dresden, I presume?" said one of the guys.

"Yes," I replied. *What? Were you expecting some other girl?*

"I'm Mr. Houghton, the head baseball coach. This is my assistant, Mr. Davenport."

I shook everyone's hand. "Nice to meet you. Thanks so much for this opportunity."

"You are more than welcome, Miss Dresden," said Houghton. "We were just taking a look at some of your game tapes, courtesy of Mr. Sabatini. Very impressive."

"Thank you," I said.

"Have a seat, Miss Dresden."

I sat in the only remaining folding chair. "You guys can call me Taylor, or just Dresden. The whole 'Miss' thing is weirding me out."

Coach Houghton laughed. "We'll try Dresden, but the administration has a thing against first names around here."

"You'll get used to it," Davenport said.

"Yeah, I guess."

"Since it's the off-season for baseball, we're going to set up a training program for you," said Houghton. "Coach Davenport runs the fitness program for the players and prospective players. It's after school every Monday, Wednesday, and Thursday, starting this week. He will give you a list of weight—" He paused and turned to Sabatini. "Hold it. Are we doing a weight program for her?"

"Why wouldn't we?" Sabatini asked.

Oh my gosh, I thought. *He's going to say it.*

"'Cause she's a girl."

Ugh.

Sabatini and Davenport looked uncomfortable. Davenport spoke first. "Girls can do weight programs, Coach. They just don't lift what the boys usually lift."

What a bunch of idiots. I could out-lift some of the boys at my old school. But I kept it polite. "I've lifted before."

"Oh good," said Houghton. "So Mr. Davenport will explain that part to you, and he'll also take you down on the team bus to the indoor practice facility at the baseball academy once a week to work on your technique with Tom Madison, our pitching coach. The students call it the bubble—it's great for winter training."

"You have a coach just for pitching?" I said.

He nodded. "Tom was in the minors with the Phillies for a few years. Never made it to the big leagues, but he really knows his stuff."

"That sounds great." I paused. "Do you guys get many college scouts here?"

"We get so many that, by the first game of the season, you'll be sick of them."

"Really? I was just asking 'cause my dad is always wondering about stuff like that." I didn't want to sound like I was using them.

"All right, Dresden, stop by if you have any more questions."

I got up and again shook everyone's hand. "I will. Thank you." I walked out of the office floating. An actual pitching coach who was a former minor leaguer—this was great. Nothing could ruin my day.

I pushed open the double doors to exit the gym and turned right at the corner of the hallway. There was Sam Barrett. *Spoke too soon,* I thought.

He was going to the gym for his meeting with the coaches. But I got what he was thinking. He was captain of the team, and he didn't want a girl playing on it. I felt the need to mess with him, since I knew he found me so revolting. I decided to be overly friendly and make him uncomfortable—a trick I'd learned years ago, and one that seemed to work real well.

"Oh, hey, are you headed in to see Coach Houghton?" I asked with a huge grin.

He was taken aback, stunned I had spoken to him when he had made it clear he was sickened by my presence in his school. "Uh, yeah," he said, quickening his pace.

"Okay, have fun!" I yelled after him in my fake happy voice. *Jerk.*

He *was* a jerk, but the whole silent treatment thing was starting to get to me. Maybe that was everyone's plan. Maybe they thought if they made me feel completely isolated, I would leave.

I guess I was lucky I was used to having only a few friends. If I had to, I could probably survive the year with just Gabby and Dr. and Mrs. Richards.

I hurried across campus back to the Richardses, swearing I would lock myself in my room with the novel I was supposed to read for English and keep reading until Gabby returned from practice. *I will study. I will study. I will study.*

I sat in the alcove of my room and cracked open the book— *The Count of Monte Cristo.* If I couldn't read in this study cubby hole, my situation was hopeless. I thought about all the smart guys who must have studied here over the last hundred years. I wondered if any of them was cute. Then I started missing Justin. It was a beautiful sunny day outside of my perfect little cubby window. *Maybe I should run instead . . . Stop it, Taylor.*

Just read.

I read a few pages, and all I got from the story was something about a large port city with a lot of people and ships. *Should I be getting more than that?* The teacher said this book was about revenge, but where was it? I read the first few chapters and I still didn't see it. It was clear that one guy was jealous of another guy named Dantés.

I became frustrated and bored, and all of a sudden anxious to hear from Gabby. It was close to six and I was getting hungry. Mrs. Richards was pretty good about having everything ready by six.

Suddenly, I heard Gabby running up the stairs. I hustled to my door.

"Hey, Gabby." I caught her as she was going by my door. "How was practice?"

She looked really upset as she stormed by me and into her room, slamming the door so hard it popped back open.

"Not good?" I asked quietly and nervously. *What's wrong with her?* She was usually so upbeat. I followed her and tapped on her door. "You okay?" I said, standing outside her door with my hand flat against it. The door was slightly ajar, and I could see her throwing clothes into a suitcase. "Wait! What are you doing?" I pushed the door open. "You're leaving?"

A teary-eyed Gabby was dialing her cell with one hand and packing with the other. "Well, I sure as hell ain't staying here!"

"Who are you calling?"

Whoever it was answered. "Baby, you need to come pick me up, now. I am so done with this place." She paused and listened. "I'm fine. I'll tell you when you get here." Another pause. "Yeah, uh-huh. I'll meet you downtown." She was still throwing things into the suitcase. "Bye. Love you, too."

I was dumbfounded. *What in the world is going on?* "Gabby, what happened?"

She slammed the suitcase shut. "I'll send my mom for the rest of this stuff," she said quickly, walking toward me.

But I blocked her with an arm extended across the doorway. "You can't just leave without telling me why," I said, trying to be as calm as possible. I was genuinely concerned, and scared to be left here all alone.

She got really close to my face. "Whatever they say I did, it's a lie, Taylor. Just remember, it's a damn lie," she said through gritted teeth. And then she pushed my arm down and flew by me.

"Gabby, wait!" I yelled, running after her, only to have the front door slammed in my face.

"Girls?" Mrs. Richards called from the kitchen. She came out wiping her hands on a dish towel. "What's all the commotion?"

I stood there looking at the front door. "Gabby left," I said.

"Left for what?"

"Left school. Quit."

"What do you mean? She left campus?" Mrs. Richards asked, very confused. She opened the front door, but Gabby was already out of sight.

Chapter 7

The rest of that early evening rushed past like a kind of a blur. Dr. Rich was on the phone most of the time making calls to the headmaster, the athletic director, the coaches, and Gabby's family, to try to figure out what had happened. Although I was dying to know, I just hung out in my room with the door cracked, hoping to overhear something that would make it clear why Gabby had stormed out. Around eight o'clock, Dr. Rich called me down to his den.

"Have a seat, Taylor," he said, escorting me into his office. He was the only adult on campus who didn't follow the last-name-only rule. I sat in the big leather wingback chair in front of his desk. He was sitting on the edge of his desk, instead of in his chair, with his arms folded across his chest. He let out a deep sigh. "Unfortunately, it seems that Gabby made some poor choices during her short time here at Hazelton."

Great! He's going to phrase this whole thing in adult talk and not come out with it. "What does that mean?" I asked.

"Well, Gabby was caught stealing from the coaches' office."

"Stealing?" I said. I hadn't known Gabby that long, only a week, but that didn't sound like her. At least, I didn't think it did. "What was she stealing?"

Dr. Rich paced around and sat down behind his desk. "Money. There was a locked cash box in the coaches' desk, and somehow she managed to get the key. Mr. Sabatini caught her opening the box after practice."

Why would she risk losing her scholarship? "Are you sure it was her?"

"It's her word against that of Mr. Sabatini and the assistant basketball coach. I'm sorry that you lost a housemate. It looked like you and Gabby were becoming friends. I just want to make sure *you're* not thinking about leaving."

"No, I wasn't thinking of it." I was so confused. "Should I be thinking of that?"

"Absolutely not. I want to be sure this whole incident doesn't change your mind about staying here."

I shook my head. "No, no, I'm not going anywhere."

He smiled. "Wonderful. Goodnight then, Taylor."

I spent the next few days trying not to think about Gabby. I had a strange feeling about her leaving. The whole thing was so sudden and strange, and deep down I thought Dr. Rich either didn't tell me, or didn't know, the whole story. I was beginning to wonder if things at Hazelton were not what they seemed to be. Maybe that Abernathy case was a bigger deal than I first suspected.

I sat in my blue room one night after dinner and decided to see what I could find on the internet about the lawsuit. I googled the name "Abernathy," but the screen read, "Site Blocked." I had noticed this before about the internet at Hazelton. They had a lot of blocked sites, including YouTube and Facebook. I guess they didn't want kids wasting their time using the internet for anything fun. I tried a few more times but got nowhere. I gave up and instead sent an e-mail to Justin and my brother Dan, and then went to bed. At least my e-mail worked.

For the first week, I had been too nervous to pick my head up and really look closely at anything. But after the incident with Gabby, I figured I should be on my toes. Maybe people were expecting me to do something, too, because of what Gabby did.

I began to watch the boys in the hall. The hall was always a sea of blue and khaki. Some of the boys were tall and thin, some short, some rushing down the hall afraid to be tardy, some hanging at their lockers like they would someday be crowned princes.

Sometimes, the perfectness of it all made me want to laugh, as if I was tarnishing the perfect-schoolboy setting merely with my presence. I again began to question why the school invited Gabby or me or any of us there in the first place. Were people really that charitable? Everyone here at Hazelton, it seemed, was always trying to impress someone else. I didn't feel that "open our doors to girls in need of a better life" aura. And as the days dragged on, I was getting more and more homesick for a place where I knew I was welcome.

I tried to overcome my homesickness by diving head-first into my workout program. On my first day with the assistant coach, Coach Davenport, I was given a pretty rigorous workout compared to the few exercises I used to do back home. My weight program was pretty extensive, too.

At first, I wasn't sure I could keep it up. I was doing chest, shoulders, and triceps twice a week, and back, biceps, and legs on the other two days. For each body part, the coach had me doing three sets of three different exercises. They wouldn't make my muscles big and bulgy like a guy's, but he promised they'd be strong and toned, which was what I needed to increase the speed and control of my pitches.

He seemed like he knew what he was talking about, but after one workout, I was so sore that the next day I was begging Mrs. Richards for some Advil. When I passed Coach Davenport in the hall the day after my first workout, I asked if it was normal not to be able to lift my arms. He just laughed and said, "If you think it hurts today, just wait until tomorrow."

"Tomorrow the pain will be gone?" I asked, hopeful.

"No, tomorrow it will be worse."

"Thanks," I said.

The next day, I was back in the weight room for more torture and, unfortunately, the other members of the team were also there, doing their workouts. Although I had had the place to myself the first day, I assumed that, from now on, I would have company. Not that it mattered—none of them would talk to me anyway.

There were twelve guys maybe more. I tried not to stare, and acted as if I didn't notice them. I slipped my hands into my pockets when I saw them and turned on my iPod. Music made people less intimidating. Now I understood why women joined those all-ladies gyms.

I carried the workout chart the coach had given me. I sat on a black workout bench in front of the wall of mirrors, staring down at the chart, trying to remember what a lat pulldown machine looked like. The coach was not in the gym, so I was going to have to ask someone or skip the exercise. I glanced behind me to see if anyone looked friendly today. *Ugh.* Sam Barrett was standing over a guy, spotting him. *Jerk.* It was such a waste having a guy that good-looking be such a stuck-up snob.

He looked at me for a second and then, as usual, looked around me, as if I didn't exist. I noticed a guy from my Chemistry class who was kind of thin and nerdy, getting a drink from the water fountain to my left. I walked over with the chart. "Hi," I said. "Cameron, right?" It seemed to my advantage to catch people off-guard when I needed an answer.

He looked up from the fountain. "Uh, yeah?"

"Do you know which one is the lat pull-down machine?"

He looked around at the other guys, as if to get their approval to speak to me.

I got in his face and whispered, "Listen, dork, I know you think you're not supposed to talk to me, but do me a favor and just point in the general direction of the freakin' machine."

He lifted a finger and pointed to the machine right behind me.

I turned and glanced at it. *Oh, yeah. Now I remember. Thanks, doofus.*

Because the good folks at Hazleton hadn't seen fit to spend some coin on a locker room for girls, I had to change in one of the few women's bathrooms at the school. There weren't very many women at Hazelton: me, Kwan, the secretary in the office, and the old Home Economics lady. Oh, well. At least the bathrooms were clean, though they did lack showers, which would have been nice.

I threw my Evansville High sweatshirt on and walked across campus toward Dr. Rich's place. I was so beat, though, that I walked at a snail's pace. The sun shined, but it was cool out. Soon the chill of fall would set in.

A tunnel ran under one of the dorms, and I went that way for a change of scenery. When I was about halfway through the tunnel, I heard voices coming from the other side. I don't know why, but something about their tone made me stop in my tracks and listen.

"Yeah, I'm thinking we go bigger with the next one," said the first voice.

"Gotta admit, girl number one was almost too easy. I still can't believe she let herself get set up like that," said the second voice.

Did he say "she"? Do they mean Gabby? They must. They must mean Gabby. "Girl number one?" Are me and Kwan next? I knew Gabby didn't steal. I knew it.

But how did she get blamed? What did they do to her? It was so hard to resist jumping out of the tunnel and screaming at them, but now was not the time. I flattened myself against the wall as best I could and listened.

"I think Mike would be proud we're doing this for him," a third party said. "So, Sam, who do we get next?"

Sam Barrett. Of course he's behind all this. He's behind everything.

"Guys, listen to me. Be patient. You can't rush things. If we really want to get back at the school for expelling McCarthy, we have to do it smoothly. You can't be too obvious or the headmaster will know you're up to something," Sam said coolly.

Man, what I wouldn't give to hit that guy. But who the heck is Mike McCarthy?

"Right. You're right, Captain. Tuttle and I will come up with a plan."

"All right, gentlemen, I have some studying to attend to. Good luck."

These guys were anything but gentlemen. They were a bunch of jackasses dressed in fancy shirts. I stayed in the tunnel for a while, still leaning against the wall. I needed to make sure no one knew I was listening. Once I was sure the coast was clear, I still couldn't get my feet to move. I slid down and sat on the concrete bottom. *Why is this happening? Why can't anything be easy for me?*

I tried to figure out what I should do, but all I kept coming up with was calling my dad and getting the hell out of Hazelton as soon as possible. Panicked, I took out my cell phone and called him.

"Hey, honey," he said.

"Hi, Dad," I said sadly.

"What's wrong, sweetheart?"

"What makes you think something is wrong?"

"'Cause you sound like you just gave up a home run in the bottom of the ninth."

"I'm just beginning to think this isn't the place for me," I said.

"Is this about Gabby?"

"How do you know about that?"

"Dr. Richards called and gave me an update," Dad said. "He said he was just keeping me in the loop."

"I guess that's part of it." I didn't want to tell my dad that she was framed, or that I might be the next target. I hated to worry him.

"Listen, sweetie, don't let one little bump in the road throw you off. I know you're not a quitter. You're a closer."

I sighed. "Dad, enough with the baseball metaphors, okay?"

"Sorry, force of habit," he said. He paused. "But it's true. You're not the quitting type."

No matter how much I wanted him to pick me up right now, it was important to make my dad proud. "Okay, Dad. Thanks for listening," I said. "I'm gonna run."

"Studying to do, right?"

"Yep," I lied.

"Love you, sweetie."

"You, too. Bye, Dad."

I remained slumped in the tunnel. I stared at my phone, which I still gripped in my hand. I could call him back right now and tell him to come get me. I could just pack up and leave and go back to my old high school—you know, the one whose baseball team I'd quit. I was heading for a job at the local Wawa, slicing deli meat, where everyone would know what a big failure I was.

I couldn't go back. I couldn't give up without a fight. My dad was right. I was not a quitter.

And just like that, I was up on my feet.

The first thing I was going to do was tell Dr. Rich about what I'd heard. Maybe he could put a stop to it and get Gabby back. I knew I'd been wrong, thinking the Abernathy lawsuit had something to do with my silent treatment. I had to find out who Mike McCarthy was, and why I was paying for what he did. Maybe Dr. Rich would tell me, since none of the students talked to me.

I entered the Richardses' kitchen and found Mrs. Richards cooking spaghetti. "Hey, Taylor. How was your day?" she asked sweetly.

"Uh, okay, I guess," I said, trying to hide how upset I was. I needed to talk to Dr. Rich, and fast. "Is Dr. Rich around?"

"He should be home shortly." She buttered a piece of bread and handed it to me. "Hungry?"

I took it, even though I was too nauseated to eat.

"I'm really sorry Gabby is gone. I know it must be hard for you, being the only girl stuck here with us," she said, dumping a box of spaghetti into the boiling pot on the stove.

"Oh, that's fine. I like it here. You guys have been great to me," I said, deciding to hit her up for more information before Dr. Rich came home. "But could I ask you something?"

"Sure." She stirred a small pot of tomato sauce.

"I heard some guys in the gym talking about a guy named Mike McCarthy. Who is he?"

She didn't seem surprised by my question. She answered calmly. "Mike McCarthy was thrown out of school last year. I think the official reason was leaving campus after curfew," she said. She put the spoon down lightly on the counter. "Hazelton is pretty strict about rules whose violation jeopardizes a kid's safety."

So maybe these guys are just pissed their friend got pinched.

"He was a pretty popular guy. Lots of kids miss him," she said.

"Oh," I said, letting it all sink in. Maybe his expulsion was enough to piss off a bunch of spoiled, rich brats. Though something felt missing from Mrs. Richards's explanation, maybe Dr. Rich could fill me in later, so I didn't press.

While I waited for Dr. Rich's arrival, I figured I'd at least find out what had really happened to Gabby, and let her know that I knew she was telling the truth.

Gabby had given me her cell number that first day. I was uncomfortable calling her. It wasn't just because of what I had overheard, but because I had never called her before. I wasn't sure if we were good enough friends, since we had only known each other a week and I would probably never see her again. Nonetheless, I hit *send.*

After two rings, I got a brusque "Hello?" She sounded annoyed.

"Hi, Gabby." I was going to say, "It's Taylor," but I knew that she knew that, so I just took a pause. "I just wanted to make sure you were okay." *And I'm afraid they're coming after me next and I need your help, so please tell me what happened.*

"Uh, yeah, I'm okay. Least I'm home and things are back to normal."

She didn't sound okay. I wasn't sure what to say, so I just let it come out. "Listen, I just want you to know I know you didn't steal anything and—"

"Damn right I didn't," she said, cutting me off.

I continued. "I overheard some of the guys talking about setting you up and I was hoping you could tell me what happened exactly."

"What's the point, Taylor? It's done now."

"I was going to tell Dr. Rich about it and I thought, maybe . . . Don't you want to come back?" I said.

"I wouldn't come back for a million dollars," Gabby said. "I don't want to spend one more minute with those fools."

"Can you just tell me what happened? Did they say anything about a guy named Mike?"

"What? No. Listen, what good will it do you to hear all this?"

I wasn't sure if she would care that I was next on the chopping block, but I gave it a shot. "I think they're going to try to set me up next, and I just want to avoid it if I can."

"What do you mean?" Gabby said. She sounded shocked. "What makes you think that?"

"They called you 'girl number one.' I assume that means me and Kwan are next."

"Why would they want to get rid of you?"

"I guess because we have breasts—same reason they didn't want you here. It's an all-boys club, and we're uninvited."

She paused for a few moments, and then said, "I thought it was because I'm black." There was relief in her voice.

"You sound happy to hear they're gunning for me and Kwan," I said, now feeling confused myself.

"No, I'm not happy. But I thought they did it because they didn't want a black person playing with them. That's all," she said. "Kind of restores my faith in humanity."

"Humanity? What about equal rights for women?"

"Yeah, I know. I'm sorry they're after you. I don't mean to downplay what could happen to you. I just always feel black before I feel female. I guess that's hard for you to understand."

There was no way for me to completely understand what Gabby was feeling, but I knew how it felt to be isolated. "My dad always says everyone has to walk in their own shoes," I said, "which I translate as everybody has crap to deal with. It's just that different people have different crap."

Gabby half-laughed and said, "Never thought about it like that. You got a point, I guess." There was warmth in Gabby's usually tough voice. "So what are we going to do about not letting those boys get the best of you?"

"Let me talk to Dr. Rich and see what he says first. Maybe he can at least clear your name, even if you don't want to come back."

"Okay," said Gabby. "Call me back ASAP."

After the call ended, I heard Dr. Rich coming through the front door. I hustled down to greet him. "Can we talk?" I said, reaching the bottom step slightly out of breath.

"Of course," he said, leading me toward his office. Upon entering the wood-paneled room, he tossed his jacket over the leather wingback chair and sat down behind his desk. "So what seems to be the trouble, Taylor?" he said, looking concerned.

I took a deep breath and tried to settle myself before speaking, so the words wouldn't come out so fast they would tackle one another. "Gabby didn't do it," I said confidently.

"What?" he said.

I picked up the pace. "I heard some guys talking outside today by the dorms, and they didn't know I was there. They were joking about how they set Gabby up, and they were talking about how they were going to get rid of me and Tara."

Dr. Rich's face twisted into confusion. "Set Gabby up? Taylor, I know you're upset about Gabby, but is it possible you misinterpreted what the boys were talking about?"

He doesn't believe me. "Who else could they be talking about?" I said, thinking it silly I'd have to defend myself.

"I'm unclear about that at this point," he said. "Let's start over. Who did you hear exactly? Do you know who the boys were?"

Yes, yes I do. "I know one was Sam Barrett, and I also heard the name Tuttle. I'm not sure who the third guy was."

He looked suddenly serious. "Sam Barrett has an outstanding reputation at Hazelton. His family is a legacy here. I doubt he would be up to anything suspicious. Maybe what you overheard was what we call around here 'boys being boys,'" he said. "Did you ever hear Gabby's name mentioned . . . or your own, for that matter?"

"Not exactly," I said, feeling defeated.

"Listen, Taylor, I'm glad you came to me with this, but I think I should share something with you that might make you choose to distance yourself from what happened with Gabby." "What do you mean?" I was confused.

He reached into his desk and removed a manila file folder. He opened it and began, "These are your records from your previous school. I have read them, as has Dr. Colton, so we are both aware of your history."

"My history?"

"I am not telling you this to upset you, but we do know that you were in counseling your freshman year, and it says here you had a history of violent behavior, specifically vandalism."

Oh my god. That's in a file? I never thought anyone else would know. I thought it was just between me and my guidance counselor.

When I was just starting high school, having had a little too much to drink, I hurled a brick through the window of my school's new science building. It was the first and last time I'd had alcohol, and I'd never done anything like it since. My counselor was the only one who knew about it, and he never involved the police, but I guess he wrote something down at some point during our sessions. It was just one bad night from my past that I thought would stay in the past. And here I was, having to explain it.

"Sir, that was a really long time ago, and I'm not like that anymore. Also, it was just one—"

"Taylor, you don't need to explain. You're not in trouble; we knew about this before we invited you here," said Dr. Rich. "I just wanted you to know that the headmaster knows about it, and if I were you, I would not want to be associated, in even a minor way, with any other criminal acts."

"Like stealing," I said.

"Precisely."

I thought about all he had said, but I still knew something was up with Barrett and Tuttle. I believed Gabby, but I couldn't risk Dr. Colton not believing me. I couldn't risk my scholarship.

And judging from what Dr. Rich said, I wasn't going to get support from the headmaster anyway. "Okay, Dr. Rich," I said, "I get what you're saying."

He pushed away from his desk and put the file back in the drawer. "I'm sure the boys don't mean either you or Miss Kwan any harm. All right?"

I nodded. "Thanks for listening," I said, then sulked out of the room. Maybe I had blown everything out of proportion. Not that it mattered. He didn't believe me anyway.

I went back to my room and called Gabby back. I sighed when she answered. "He didn't believe me," I said, leaving out the part about my screwed-up past.

"Kind of figured something like that would happen."

"So now what?" I asked.

"What are you doing tomorrow night?" she asked suddenly.

"Uh, the usual. Not studying," I said.

"I'll meet you downtown. There's a little restaurant by the square."

"Rodman's?" I asked.

"Yeah. I'll have Jordan drive me over. Like seven o'clock?" she said in a serious tone.

"Okay."

"See ya then," she said.

"Oh, wait, Gabby."

"Yeah?"

"Thanks."

Chapter 8

The next morning, I realized I had a bigger, more immediate problem than being set up and tossed out of Hazelton, or being embarrassed about the headmaster knowing about my vandalism incident. I had to keep from flunking out. I had conveniently forgotten about my first quiz in Trig—well, not completely forgotten. I remembered all of a sudden when Mr. Moesch said, "Clear your desks." *Oops.* This was going to be bad, as in, "I'll be lucky if I spell my name right" kind of bad.

I stared down at the ten problems in front of me. *Why haven't I studied? Why can't I get serious?* The whole reason my dad wanted me to come to this snotty two-faced prep school was so I could get into a good college, and here I was, making the same old mistakes. *I'm going to make it easy for these guys to get rid of me.*

I looked around after a few minutes and cracked my knuckles out of nervous habit. Ben Barrett heard me, looked back at me, and smiled. I didn't react. What a big phony, acting like we're friends when he and his buddies and his evil twin were trying to get rid of me!

I tried to write something down, but I honestly had no clue what. Eventually, I just started doodling at the bottom of the quiz sheet. It seemed like hours passed before I heard the sweet sound of the bell ringing to end the period. I put the quiz in the basket on Mr. Moesch's desk and skulked out of the room.

I then found myself in the hall, face to face with William Tuttle. He was one of the guys I had overheard the day before in the tunnel. He was on the short side, with short blond hair that spiked up in the front. He gave me a big smile with Tom Cruise teeth too large for his small mouth. "Taylor, right?" he said, blocking my way to my next period class. "How'd you do on the quiz?"

"Sorry, late for class," I said, squeezing against the wall to get by him. Although Dr. Rich had told me I was wrong to think the boys were gunning for me, I trusted my instinct. And I knew Tuttle was a pitcher, which I'm sure added fuel to his fire. I had no intention of being nice or showing him I could be manipulated. I decided to be intentionally rude. "'Scuse me."

I caught a glimpse of his face as I slipped past. He was caught way off-guard—obviously stunned that I had snubbed a popular senior who hung with the Barrett boys. I figured if I never talked to him, maybe I could avoid his evil plan to take me down.

As I walked down the hall, I felt slightly bad for my rudeness. Maybe he was just wondering how I did on the quiz. But then again, I couldn't be too careful.

After school that day, I worked out in the gym and kept my eyes open. Although Dr. Rich had told me to distance myself from Gabby, I decided to meet her at Rodman's. What could it hurt?

I arrived at Rodman's right at seven that night. I had borrowed a bike from Mrs. Richards that had been left in her garage by a former student. I put it on the nearest bike rack and hoped everyone was feeling honest—I hadn't brought a lock. As I was parking the bike, a long black car pulled up beside the curb; it looked like the used Cadillac my grandpa used to drive. I was relieved to see it was Gabby.

"Hey, Dresden," she said, leaning out of the passenger-side window.

"Hey, thanks for coming." I bent forward and leaned into the car window.

"Taylor, this is my boyfriend, Jordan."

I crouched down further and rested my arms on the window. "Hey, Jordan," I said. "Nice to meet you."

He nodded, smacking a pack of cigarettes repeatedly against his palm.

"You guys want to go in and grab something to eat?" I asked.

"No, there may be Hazelton guys in there, and if I see one, I may have to hold Jordan back." Jordan nodded again and turned the radio down so we could talk. Gabby got out of the car and leaned against it.

"Listen, Taylor, I don't have much to tell you," she said. "That day after practice, this guy on the team—Grossman was his name—he unlocked the ladies' restroom for me so I could change. He handed me a key and asked me to please return it to the top right-side drawer in the coaches' office when I was finished. So after I dressed, I went into the office and opened the drawer. The coaches came in and asked me how I got the key to the lockbox. I didn't know what they were talking about. That's when I knew I'd been set up." She shook her head. "I tried to explain, but he must have switched keys. The one he left me with was the one that opened their cash box."

I crossed my arms. "I'm sorry, Gabby."

"Why? *You* didn't do it."

"I know. I just feel bad that it happened. I know how much you wanted to play ball here."

"It's cool. I'm fine, and they'll lose every game without me. Right, baby?" she said to Jordan.

"You know it," Jordan said.

"So did the school call the police?"

"No, that's the weird thing about it. The coach who came in and thought I was stealing said to go back to Dr. Rich's house, and he would have the headmaster send for me," she said. "But I just picked up and left. Later that night, the headmaster called my mom."

"What did he say?"

"He said I could come back to school on probation if I put an apology in writing to the coaches and the students."

"But you didn't want to do that?"

"What the hell do I have to apologize for?" she said.

"True," I said quickly. "It's weird they were willing to let someone back who they thought stole from the school. I heard something on TV about our being here having to do with some lawsuit. I wonder if that's why." I paused. "You sure you don't want to come back?"

"No. No way. They don't deserve me."

"Their loss."

"Totally," she said.

"What would you do if you were me?" I said.

"Just watch your back. At least you know what's going on. Maybe you can avoid them or something. And maybe you should give that Kwan girl a heads-up."

"Yeah, maybe," I said, "and if there's any way I can get back at them for what they did to you, Gabby, trust me, I will."

She gave me a quick hug. "Just take care of yourself. And keep in touch. E-mail me if you need anything."

"Okay. Thanks for driving down here," I said.

"No problem," she said, climbing back into the car.

I waved at the car and watched it drive away. As I turned toward the bike rack, I noticed a group of guys sitting on the steps outside of Rodman's, looking in my direction. When I got on my bike, they quickly stood up and got into a nearby car. It was an old brown Mercedes with a rag top. The driver, I recognized, was William Tuttle. *Did they see me talking to Gabby? Do they know that I know?*

I turned onto Nassau Street and headed toward Hazelton. The sun was beginning to set and the sky was darkening. I heard a car approaching. I was afraid to look back to see if it was Tuttle and his guys. I stayed focused on the road ahead, fighting my urge to look back. The car wasn't passing me, and it should have passed me by now. I had to peek.

And there it was. The brown Mercedes.

Tuttle was driving, and three other guys were with him. In the backseat, I recognized Ben Barrett and the evil Sam Barrett. The car was only a few feet behind me, just riding along. None of them was looking at me. They were just staring straight ahead, the car radio blasting some hard rock, and maintaining the same distance from me.

It continued like that for a long time. If I pedaled faster, they sped up. If I slowed down, they slowed down. My heart began to race. *What should I do?*

After about a quarter mile, I turned onto a long, private

driveway and pedaled up toward an unknown house. Tuttle and his boys didn't follow. Tuttle sped up and I watched his car cruise out of sight. I stopped in the driveway and caught my breath. I wiped the sweat off my forehead. After a few more cars passed, I ventured back onto the road. I pedaled as fast as I could back to campus, the whole time wondering what they were thinking of doing to me.

That night, my dad called. He told me how he had told all his friends at work that I was attending Hazelton. He sounded so happy and proud. I couldn't bear to tell him that I wanted to come home, and that everyone here hated me.

After I hung up, I determined that I had to make it through the year at Hazelton, for two reasons: one, to make my dad proud; and two, to stick it to these guys for what they'd done to Gabby—maybe even get revenge like that count of Monte Cristo character did in the book. Of course, I'd only read the first few chapters, so I didn't know how he did it yet, but I'd think of something. As long as I stayed on my toes, what was the worst that could happen?

The next day, I figured I should make good on one of the promises I made to Gabby and warn Tara Kwan. I didn't usually see her during school hours because she was a sophomore. During sophomore lunch, I excused myself from Chemistry, telling the teacher I had to use the ladies' room, and walked quickly toward the café, where the nearest ladies' room was located. I spotted Kwan at a small table in the back, holding an apple in one hand and a book in the other.

I knew I had only a few minutes to explain. I tried to gather my thoughts as I approached her, so as not to sound like an overbearing lunatic. "Hi, Tara," I said. "Mind if I sit?"

She looked surprised to hear a voice, but said, "No, go ahead."

I told her what I knew—that Gabby was set up. "These guys—I think they're all seniors—framed her, and I'm pretty sure they're trying to get rid of us, too." I paused. "Me and you," I said, pointing to the two of us. By the look on her face, I realized I had failed in my attempt not to sound like a lunatic.

Kwan wrinkled her brow. "So someone is going to frame me?" she said in the slow-paced kind of voice that people use when they think they're talking to a crazy person.

"Yes! Well, maybe. I don't know, just . . ." I was starting to realize this was not working and sighed. "Just be careful." I got up quickly, because I knew I was taking too long. "If anything weird happens, let me know."

Kwan just sat silently and stared at me.

"All right, see ya around," I said before bailing out of the café. *Ugh, that went well,* I thought as I raced back to class. But at least I'd tried to help her. *For the time being, I guess I'll just focus on helping myself.*

Chapter 9

Working out became my life over the next month. I would get up every morning at six and go for a run, usually about two miles. Every other day, I would go to the gym to lift, and on Wednesdays, I would go to the practice bubble to meet with Tom Madison, the pitching coach.

I blocked out the fact that no one in the school would talk to me. I tried not to let it bother me. Gabby and I had developed an online chat and text message relationship, and my dad became my phone buddy whenever I needed a live voice. I became kind of immune to the head-turns and lack of social relations with the boys at school. I focused on becoming physically stronger, and that helped keep me sane. Any time I was feeling alone, I just took a longer run, or threw a little harder, or lifted more weight.

My first day training with Madison inspired me to become a gym rat. I was so happy to be pitching again, because I hadn't thrown in about a month. The indoor practice bubble was the coolest thing I had ever seen. It was a whole baseball field minus the stands, with a foggy plastic dome covering everything. It reminded me of where professional football teams practiced. I sat on one of the side benches and waited for Madison, Sabatini, and Davenport to finish up with another pitcher, my favorite person, William Tuttle.

As I watched Tuttle, I had to admit he was good—but to be honest, I knew I was better. Most high school varsity teams, like Hazelton, usually have two starting pitchers, and a third guy who could come in as a reliever. And there were always a couple outfielders who could throw a few if necessary.

I had always been a reliever, but I really wanted one of the starter spots. My old coaches wouldn't start me. I threw so hard, they worried about me hurting myself. But now, I was older and stronger. I could be a starter and I wanted it bad. It was obvious that Tuttle did, too. When we exchanged places on the bench, I avoided looking him in the eye, but I knew his eyes were on me.

I was so happy to be pitching again, I was able to shut him out.

I could tell that Madison was impressed with me when he saw me warming up.

"Uh-oh. Tom's got that twinkle in his eye," Sabatini said to the assistant coach as I threw a few fastballs.

Madison jogged out onto the mound. "Taylor, good to meet you."

I put the ball in my glove, wiped my hand on my sweats, and shook his hand. "You, too."

"I'm just going to stand behind you and watch you throw a couple, okay?"

"Sure."

"Davenport, get the gun on these next few."

I had never really had anyone measure the speed of my pitches. My high school had zero technology.

"Taylor, just throw a couple fastballs."

The coach directed a Hazelton guy to catch me. All I knew

was that his last name was Roberts. He crouched down behind the plate only because the coach had ordered him to. He said nothing to me. *Jerk!*

I fired a few right down the middle. With each one, the assistant coach yelled out a number: "Seventy-four! Seventy-one! Seventy-eight!"

"Is that good?" I didn't know, but the look on Sabatini's and Madison's faces made me believe it was.

"What's good is that you can throw that fast and still put it in the catcher's mitt," said Madison.

"Not all strikes, though."

"Don't worry, we'll work on that."

And for the next month, we did. Coach Madison showed me how important it was to develop my muscles so I could gain full range of motion. He showed me how to gain greater control over my pitches. The day I met him, I knew right away I would learn a lot from him. He was kind to me, and never commented about me being a girl. Spending time with him made the silent treatment I was dealing with a little more bearable.

For most of the major holidays, Hazelton held a student dance. The first one of the year was for Halloween. The girls from the nearby private schools were all invited, and any Hazelton boy could bring one guest. This was usually the time the guys who had girlfriends from home brought them around, but mostly it was the unattached guys trying to get a good night of action from the girls.

Mrs. Richards hassled me all week about whether or not

I was going. I figured if no one talked to me at school or in the gym, donning a dress for them wouldn't make a world of difference.

Nevertheless, at dinner that Friday, the night the dance was being held, both Dr. and Mrs. Richards were laying on me that "you should go and be social" guilt trip. Somehow, it worked. The dance was taking place in the gym, and I decided to get dressed and go over for an hour, just to humor them, since they had been so nice to me.

I had brought only one decent dress outfit from home. It was a black spaghetti-strap dress I'd bought that summer to go to Justin's cousin's wedding. I slipped it on and looked at myself in the mirror. It was a little tighter around the straps than the last time I had worn it and, standing back, I noticed how much bigger my arms and shoulders had gotten from all the conditioning. I looked really fit, and I liked the look.

Because it was getting cooler out, I decided a sweater was necessary. I wasn't sure how comfortable I felt showing this much skin anyway. Besides, it would be best if I didn't look like my usual self, so I could blend in with the girls from the other schools. I left my hair down and even made an attempt at using Mrs. Richards's curling iron. I put on lip gloss and a decent amount of makeup. Maybe nobody would recognize me, and someone might actually talk to me.

By the time I got to the gym, it was packed. It was so weird to see girls mixing with the boys. Of course, the one girl I kind of knew, Kwan, was not there. I found out later that her parents were really strict and wouldn't allow her to attend.

A lot of people were out on the dance floor looking like idiots, as the DJ played top-forty dance songs. I don't dance— not fast-dance, anyway. On occasion, I had slow-danced with

Justin just to please him, but it always made me feel really stupid—like I wasn't sure what to do.

Having gone on a three-mile run earlier in the evening, I was starving, so I hunted down the food table, where I found a couple chocolate cookies and a Diet Coke. Chocolate and caffeine made getting dressed and coming over to the dance all worthwhile. The Richardses never had sweets, and my secret stash of soda had run out a few weeks ago. I cracked open the can of soda and put it down at the end of the table so I could gnash down my cookies.

"You shouldn't eat cookies when you're training," a voice said from behind the table.

It was Ben Barrett, the lesser evil twin, who hadn't spoken to me since the first day of classes. Maybe he was off-duty from shunning me—it was, after all, a special event. I let my guard down.

"I figure I'll run it off tomorrow."

"I almost didn't recognize you in that dress," he said, smiling.

Should I be talking to him? "Yeah, well, I'm full of surprises."

"Yeah, Chalky says you have quite a curve ball."

"Who's Chalky?" I said.

"Uh, short, kind of heavyset guy," said Ben. "Said he caught for you at the bubble last week."

"Oh, is his last name Roberts?"

"Yeah, that's him."

"How do you get Chalky from Roberts?"

"His first name's Charles. Everyone around here has a nickname."

I reached back for my Diet Coke and took a swig. Under my breath, I said, "I can just imagine what mine is."

"Excuse me?" he asked.

I shook my head. "Just talking to myself."

"Hey, Benny!" a girl exclaimed, skipping toward us. Blonde and super preppy, she had "rich girl" written all over her.

"Claire, how are you?" he asked, giving her a hug.

I took my cookie, exited the happy reunion, and sat down at one of the round tables. There were a few other girls there I said hello to, but the music was so loud, it was kind of pointless to say more. I looked at the big clock on the wall. It was 7:25. I'd promised myself, for the sake of the Richardses, that I would stay a whole hour, so I had to hang out for another half hour or so. I scanned the room for something to do and drank my soda. I figured I'd just do some people-watching.

The girls were all very pretty. By the way their nails were done, not to mention their expensive shoes and their occasional diamonds, it was clear they had money. But they weren't tacky or overdone like some of the girls back home. They looked classy.

A slow song came on, and the couples formed. In the distance, I could see Ben dancing with his friend Claire. That Tuttle guy was across the gym surrounded by a group of his cronies, laughing. They were probably discussing how to get rid of me. I wondered how much time I had left before they tried something.

And then I spotted the other Barrett—Sam Barrett. He was dancing with a girl not too far away from me. He held her at enough of a distance that I could see he wasn't that into her. She was a lot shorter than he was, and had glasses and long curly brown hair that swayed as they danced. Maybe she was a cousin, or a friend. I would think Sam "The Captain" Barrett could do better than that.

He looked my way and caught me staring. *Oops!* Still, I didn't look away at first. I stared back for a while, wanting to flip him off or stick out my tongue at him. Or maybe I kept looking his way just because he was gorgeous.

He was still looking at me. *Okay, I have to end this.* I looked to my left and finished my soda.

After a few more minutes of sitting, I had to do something, so I got up from the table and walked over to the back of the gym, toward the trash cans, to toss my soda can. Mr. Sabatini stood in the back, chaperoning and checking his Blackberry. I was going to say hello to him, but I suddenly felt kind of dizzy. *Maybe it's too hot in here. Maybe I just need some water or air.* I smiled as I passed by Mr. Sabatini and pushed through the heavy exit door. The hall was dim, but I could see the door at the end of the corridor that led outside.

I tried to walk toward it, but with every step I took, I couldn't make myself go straight. Twice, before stopping myself, I bumped into lockers on the right. I put my arm against them and tried to steady myself. Everything was spinning. *What's going on?*

I sat down on the floor and leaned my head against the lockers, still trying to focus on the door at the end of the hall. *If I could just get up.* I heard a door slam behind me and footsteps approaching. It was too dark to see who was there. All I heard was, "Come on, you've got to get up. We have to move."

And then I completely blacked out.

I woke up to the sound of coffee dripping into a pot. My head was pounding and everything looked a little blurred. My eyes were dry because I had fallen asleep with my contacts in, so it took a minute to focus. This was not my perfect blue room at the Richards house.

And then I heard someone else in the room. I peeked out from under the covers, afraid to move and let the person, whoever it was, know I was awake.

The last thing I remembered was being in the hallway outside the gym and feeling dizzy. *What in the world happened? Oh my god, someone slipped me a date rape drug!*

Suddenly, the person in the room moved into my periphery, and I could see clearly who it was—Sam Barrett. He was sitting on a black desk chair, swiveling back and forth.

I immediately sat up and scowled. "What the hell?!"

Sam grabbed his chest and almost spilled his coffee. "Oh, good, you're awake."

Only then did I realize I was wearing an unfamiliar t-shirt over my black dress, which was riding up around my waist. I pulled the covers up and wiggled my dress down toward my knees.

My head pounded, but I refused to show weakness in front of him. "You better start explaining," I said. *Oh my gosh, maybe I got loaded and hooked up with this guy. No way! He despises me as much as I despise him.*

He rolled his chair next to the bed. He leaned forward, his coffee in one hand, and pushed his hair back with the other. He looked sad, like he was about to deliver some bad news.

"I guess you had a little too much to drink at the dance last night." His face changed to its usual know-it-all sneer.

"Too much to drink? What? How did I get here?" I said. I didn't drink anything besides soda. *Or did I?*

"You wandered onto my floor and passed out in the hall. I

was going to call for help, but I didn't want to be blamed for your condition."

I hated his righteous attitude, like he was so much better than me. I got up, feeling embarrassed, and reached for my black sweater lying on the end of the bed. "If you say so," I said defensively. "What happened to my sweater?"

"Vomit happened," he said, pointing at the stain on the front.

My face burned with rage. I couldn't get out of the room fast enough. I grabbed my puked-on sweater, scooped my black shoes off the floor by the bed, and darted out of the room.

He yelled after me, "You're welcome!" as I slammed the door behind me. "And you can keep the t-shirt!"

I ran down two flights of stairs and out the exit door at the end of the stairwell. There were three dorms on campus, and I wasn't sure which one I'd just left. I stood outside in the early morning air and looked around to get my bearings. Once I realized I was standing outside of Nichols, I took the path to my left, because it would lead me back toward the Richardses' place.

How could I have let this happen? When did I drink something alcoholic? I don't remember doing that. How could I have let my guard down like that? As I approached the Richards house, I realized I had been gone all night, and that I was probably in deep crap.

Knowing the Richardses, they had called the police, as well as everyone in the school. *Oh, no. This is it. This is how I'm going to get thrown out of school. Someone must have drugged me. Sam must have drugged me. He drugged me and locked me in his room all night so I couldn't get back before curfew.* I would just have to explain to Dr. Richards that I had been drugged and held against my will. He would believe me. He had to. Right?

When I got to the Richardses' front door, it was quiet. Since the sun was just starting to come up, I figured it was probably not even six o'clock. There was no one in the foyer when I stepped inside. I tiptoed up to my room. Maybe I could at least change out of these clothes and appear somewhat presentable before the inquisition. As I crept quietly down the hall, I wondered if I should lie about where I'd been or be honest. If I was going to lie, then where would I say I'd spent the night?

I opened my bedroom door and almost shrieked. There was someone underneath my bed covers. I assumed it was a girl, because I saw long, straight brown hair sticking out on my pillow. *Who the heck is this? Should I wake her up?*

I sat in my alcove and stared briefly at her. Then I gently kicked the bed a little bit, hoping that would be enough to stir her. She sat up and looked at me. "Oh, good, you're back," she said with a yawn. She pushed off the covers and swung her legs out of the bed. She was wearing a black dress, similar to mine, and had my hair color. It was kind of freaky.

"Who are you?" I asked, keeping a safe distance from her.

"I was playing your body double until you got back."

"My body double?" I said.

"Yeah. Worked like a charm, too. Dr. Richards was watching TV in the living room, and I walked in the front door and ran up the stairs so quick he never knew the difference." She crossed the room and examined herself in the mirror.

"So they think I was here all night?"

"Uh-huh. And I better get out of here before they see me," she said, trying to smooth down her hair.

"Wait a minute. Who told you to do this?"

"Sam. Paid me fifty bucks, too," she said, slipping on her shoes.

"Sam Barrett?" I asked.

"That's the one," she said, smiling. "He's so hot I would have done it for free."

Sam paid her to pretend to be me? But doesn't he want to get me in trouble? My head was spinning.

"Okay, then, I'm going to go. Cover me, would you?" she said, opening my door.

"Huh?"

"Just stand by the door and let me know if anyone's coming," she said.

"Oh, okay." I stood by my door and watched my double sneak down the wide stairs and out the front door. *Did that really just happen?* I was too tired to think. I peeled off my clothes, throwing them on my closet floor, slipped into my black yoga pants and a clean t-shirt, and climbed into bed. There was no point thinking about any of this now, when I couldn't think clearly.

Exhaustion won out for the moment.

Chapter 10

The clock read 10:43 when I woke up. It took me a minute to realize it was Saturday morning, and to remember where I had woken up five hours earlier—in Sam Barrett's dorm room.

I sat up and tried to figure out what to do. *Should I tell someone what happened?* I got out of bed and hustled down the hall to the bathroom. I had never needed a shower more. I cranked the temperature up and stepped in.

As I showered, I thought about how Sam had said I passed out in the hallway near his room. But my mind refused to believe that story. The last place I remembered being conscious was in the hallway outside of the gym, so how could I have made it all the way across campus, into his dorm, and then up three floors to his room? That wasn't possible. Someone must have carried me up there.

I shut off the water and wrapped a towel around my hair. And then I remembered something else. I remembered someone telling me to get up. "Get up. We have to move." But who was it? What had happened to me during the hours I was out? I was afraid to even imagine.

As I got dressed, I considered what to do with the dirty pile of clothes on the closet floor. I took out Barrett's t-shirt and looked around the room for someplace to put it. I thought about throwing it away, but I worried that someone might see it, so I stuffed it into the bottom of one of my dresser drawers for the time being. The dress and sweater went into my laundry basket. Today was definitely a good day to do some laundry, so Mrs. Richards wouldn't find or smell the dress or the sweater.

When I finally got downstairs, Mrs. Richards was in the kitchen. "Hey, Taylor, you're a little late for breakfast. Would you like to have lunch with Matthew?" she said.

I was starving. "Yeah, that would be great."

"I guess this is what it's like to be a teenager, huh? Sleeping 'til noon?"

"Sorry about that. I guess I've been working out too much."

"Oh, no problem. A little extra sleep never hurt anybody. Wish this little guy would sleep in once in a while," she said, putting a cheese stick in Matthew's hand. "How was the dance?"

"Uh, okay. Not too painful."

"You were home early enough."

"Yeah. Wasn't really my scene."

As I wolfed down two grilled cheese sandwiches, Dr. Rich walked into the kitchen. "Good morning, young lady. Or should I say, 'Good afternoon'?"

"Hi," I said, still chewing.

"When you're done with lunch, come see me in the den."

I nodded as I chewed, but my stomach turned. *Uh-oh. He knows.* I quickly finished the rest of my lunch and made my way toward the den. I figured, why delay the inevitable?

"Taylor, have a seat. I want to talk to you about something."

I sat down. *Should I say something about last night before he does? Would he believe me this time?*

"I received a call this morning from your math teacher."

A different uh-oh.

"He informed me that you failed your first two quizzes. He also said he checked with your other teachers, and you're pulling just a C or so in all of your courses."

I winced. Like I needed this today.

"Now, I know that you are here on a scholarship for athletics, but in order to keep that scholarship, you have to maintain a C average or better in all your courses or, come springtime, you won't be able to play baseball. And to be honest, they may withdraw your scholarship by the end of this semester, unless your grades improve."

"Withdraw?"

"Take it away and send you back home."

I was embarrassed. Dr. Rich had been so nice to me, and I was letting him down. "I'm really sorry, Dr. Rich."

"Well, you don't have to be sorry. You just have to figure out what to do about it."

I didn't know what to say.

"So make a plan for yourself. Figure out how to bring those grades up, starting right now. Go see you teachers, and sign up for tutoring, but don't waste any time. Do something now."

"Okay, I will." But to be honest, I didn't know the first thing about buckling down and studying. I thought I had been studying these past two months, but I guess I wasn't very good at it. I was good at throwing curve balls. Couldn't they grade me on that instead?

I sulked around in my room for the next few hours. I was failing. All the boys at school had started their plan to get me thrown out. I was too tired to go for a run. I had bags underneath my eyes—at seventeen! Life sucked.

Unwilling to wait for the next bad thing to happen, I grabbed my Trig book, threw it into my book bag, and headed over to the library. Me at the library on a Saturday? How wild was that? Well, these were desperate times.

I found a place in the library's back corner. It was a big wooden desk with shelves above it, all of which created my own private cubicle. I would learn this stuff somehow, I thought, opening my notebook and the book.

Suddenly, it was hard to focus. Too much going on in my head. I wondered how many people knew about last night. I was sure Sam had told everyone. Hopefully, one of those people was not the headmaster.

Then someone dropped some books down on the other side of the desk I was using. After a few minutes, a small, folded-up piece of paper came over the top of the shelves. I was dumbfounded. I sat back in my chair, afraid to touch it. Who was passing notes to me? No one talked to me. I wasn't sure if I should pretend it wasn't there or if I should read it. But I was dying to know what it said.

I opened the note: "I need to talk to you. I need to explain what happened last night."

I pulled my Yankees hat down a little. I slowly stood up and looked over the top of the shelves. I saw the top of Sam Barrett's head. He was pretending to read. *Ugh, Barrett. I am not going to talk to that piece of crap. Ever.*

I grabbed my book and bag and quickly made for the exit in the back of the library. But before the door closed completely, there was Barrett, right on my heels.

"Dresden, wait," he said, only slightly louder than a whisper.

I kept moving up the hill toward the tunnel that went under the dorms. He followed. He ran ahead and stood in front of me, blocking my way out of the tunnel.

"Please, give me a minute to explain. I'm trying to help."

I laughed. "Help. Right. Why the hell would I believe you?"

"I know you have no reason to, but I'm telling the truth."

I sneered at him. "I know the truth, Sam. I know what you did to Gabby. And I know what you're trying to do to me. Now get out of my way." I would hit him if I had to. I had no qualms about clocking him to get by. I moved to the right and he moved with me.

"Just give me a chance, okay? Will it kill you to listen to me for one minute?" he asked, resuming his position in front of me.

"It's hard for me to give a minute to someone who had a hand in drugging me last night," I said, throwing a shoulder into him and moving him out of the way.

He grabbed me by the arm and spun me around. "I didn't drug you, Taylor."

"Then who did?!" I shouted, shaking my arm free.

"That's not important."

"It is to me."

"Listen, what's important is their plan didn't work."

"Whose plan?" I crossed my arms and finally stopped moving. Now I was curious.

He hesitated. "The Statesmen's," he said after a sigh.

"Who the hell are the Statesmen?"

"They're the guys who kind of run things around here—Tuttle, Briggs, Grossman, Phillips, a lot of guys."

"I was in the tunnel when you were celebrating your success in framing Gabby," I said. "I assumed you were part of that group."

"You heard that?" he asked, looking embarrassed.

"Yes, *Captain*, I did."

He cringed. "I'm truly sorry about your friend, but that

wasn't my decision. I swear to you."

"But you are part of the group, aren't you?"

"Yes."

"So what's your role, then? Why do they call you 'Captain'?"

He ran his fingers through his hair to push it out of his eyes. "'Cause I'm the leader."

I couldn't have been more confused. "You know that what you just said makes no sense, don't you? If you're with them, why are you trying to help me?"

"'Cause I don't want them to get rid of you. I'm done messing with people's lives. I can't do that anymore."

"Do what?"

"I've been with these guys for three years," he said. "We control everything. We decide who's popular and who isn't, even who can walk with whom in the halls. And I'm just tired of it all. I'm not going to do it anymore."

He seemed legitimately upset. I stepped back and looked at him. *This must be an act—an act to get me to trust him.* "You must belong to the Theater Club, Barrett. That was quite a performance," I said before storming off.

Chapter 11

I spent the rest of the weekend trying to forget my conversation with Sam Barrett. I'd decided he was a liar, and that was that. On Monday, I put my focus on schoolwork. I read *The Count of Monte Cristo* while I ate lunch. I carefully took notes in Chemistry.

I was waiting to hear hall gossip about my "intoxicated state" Friday night, but it seemed to be business as usual with the boys—ignore me, ignore me, ignore me. For once, the silence made me happy. It was certainly nicer than the alternative. Maybe Sam had put a stop to some drama in the making, but I wasn't going to take any chances by talking to him.

For the next few weeks, I went for extra after-school Trig help with Mr. Moesch on those days when I didn't have gym work to do. I kept to myself, studied in my alcove, and was in bed before ten each night. Report cards were going to be issued after we got back from Thanksgiving vacation, which couldn't come soon enough for me.

My dad came up on the Wednesday before Turkey Day. I fell into his arms and smiled when I saw him come through the front door of the Richardses'. I slept in the car the whole way home and didn't get up until ten the next day, waking up only because Dan came in and jumped on my head.

"T, you're home!" he said, jabbing his elbow into my side.

"Give me a break, Dan. I'm trying to sleep."

He threw a pillow at my head. "Come on, get up."

I rolled over and put the pillow over my head.

"Uh-oh, what's this?" he said, grabbing my arm. "Have you been juicing?"

"What?"

He held up my arm. I was wearing my Evansville High tank top. "Your arms are jacked. Woo!" he said. "Dad, I think Taylor is using those performance enhancing drugs over at Hazelton!" he yelled down the stairs.

"I'm not," I said, laughing. "I just don't have much to do up there except study and work out." I threw the pillow back at him.

"Come on, Hercules. We're going to Grandma's in an hour and Dad said you have to make your famous pumpkin pie."

"Dan, you know we just buy that from Wegman's, don't you?"

"Mmm. Nothing like home cooking."

"You're an idiot," I said. "Now get out so I can get dressed."

Grandma Jen's was packed with relatives. My dad had two brothers and two sisters, and I had ten cousins. They were as young as four and as old as twenty. The day was always loud and crazy, and it was just what I needed after the long first few months at Hazelton.

Over pumpkin pie, I made Hazelton sound great, and parts of it were. I told everyone how beautiful the campus and the town were and about how smart all of the teachers were, all of which was true. I raved about working with the pitching coach.

I didn't mention what had happened to Gabby, or the evil boys looking to force me out before baseball season. I didn't want to let my dad know, either. I could see the pride in his face as everyone asked me about school. I wasn't going to ruin it for him.

Later that night, I was back in my old room, online, checking e-mail. Justin and I had been e-mailing once every few weeks or so, but I hadn't written in a while. I spilled my guts to him about the situation at Hazelton. I had to tell somebody, and with him safely across the Atlantic Ocean, I figured it couldn't get back to my dad. I hit send and wondered what his advice would be. I pictured him flying back home to rescue me and challenging the Barrett boys to a duel to defend my honor. But I knew that wasn't Justin's style. He was more of a ride-it-out kind of guy, but it was nice to fantasize for a minute.

My instant message chimed, bringing me back to reality. It wasn't one of my buddies. A window popped up, asking me to accept or block the message. I didn't recognize the screen name, SJB04068. Maybe Justin had changed his name after settling in Europe. I hit accept.

SJB04068: Hi Taylor, it's Sam.

Shoot. Big mistake. And now he has my screen name! I might as well just make it easy for him and drop out of Hazelton.

TDPITCHER: What do u want?
SJB04068: Happy Thanksgiving to you too.

I didn't respond. I just leaned back in my chair and stared at the screen. Maybe he would stop sending messages if I didn't answer.

SJB04068: I was hoping we could try to talk again.

TDPITCHER: Why won't u just leave me alone?

SJB04068: I have for the past three weeks. I thought maybe you'd have cooled off by now.

I tried to be meaner.

TDPITCHER: Let me make this clear. I don't **TRUST** u and I don't want to talk to u.

SJB04068: Okay. But before I go, did you see your grades yet? They're posted on the school web page.

TDPITCHER: No. I didn't want to ruin my Thxgiving, but thanks for reminding me.

SJB04068: Listen, if you need help in Trig, I'm pretty good at it.

TDPITCHER: How'd u know about my Trig grade?

SJB04068: I told you before, I know everything that goes on at school.

TDPITCHER: Goodbye Sam.

SJB04068: Wait. Come on. Let me make up for what happened at the Halloween dance. I could help you with your math.

TDPITCHER: So u admit to drugging me now?

SJB04068: I told you before it wasn't me.

TDPITCHER: Whatever, Captain.

SJB04068: Let me tutor you and I'll tell you everything. The whole truth, I promise.

TDPITCHER: So until now u've been lying?

SJB04068: If you consider not telling the whole story lying, then yes.

TDPITCHER: Bye Sam.

I hit "sign off" and slammed the door on him. I quickly logged onto the school website to see how bad my Trig grade was. Probably anything less than an A was a bad grade to Sam Barrett, master of the universe.

And there it was, a C-minus. The minus meant my average was too low to play ball if the season started today. I had one marking period to bring it up or there was really no point staying at Hazelton. I was sure come Monday I would have to meet with the headmaster to discuss my grades. I'd probably be on probation or something. C's at Hazelton are probably like F's at my old school.

My other grades weren't as bad as I had expected: B's in English and History, a C+ in chemistry. I guess I needed some help in that subject, too. I got an A in Spanish, which wasn't difficult since I grew up in Evansville, where almost half the kids in my school were from Puerto Rico. I'd been hearing Spanish since kindergarten.

I stared at the screen. To be honest, if this were a report card from my old high school, I would have been very proud of myself. I usually didn't get anything above a C. Of course, this was also the first time I had ever really tried to study, and I felt proud of the two B's I got. I actually did read that novel for English, and I enjoyed reading it. That was probably because the guy framed by the people he most trusted breaks out of prison and gets revenge on all of them.

A pop-up came on the screen telling me I had a new e-mail. I opened it. It was a reply from Justin. He wrote just a few sentences, but it was enough to make me feel better.

T,

These guys sound weak. You're stronger than all their crap. You'll be fine. You always are. I'm here if you need me.

Keep in touch,

J

Maybe I could turn this thing around on the boys at school. Maybe I could get them before they got me. *Hmm, doubtful.*

I was curious about what Sam meant by not telling me the whole truth. What had happened that night? It was a horrible thing not to know what I was doing for all those hours, only to wake up confused in the enemy's dorm room.

I could meet with Sam just to find out what happened. I would have to be careful, though. I should set the time and place, and not give him much notice, so he wouldn't have time to inform the stupid Statesmen.

On the ride back up to Hazelton that Sunday night, I had a long talk with my dad. I hadn't planned on it, but he brought it up.

"So, what are we going to do about that C-minus in math?" he said.

"I was afraid you were going to ask me about that."

"Truth is, honey, you've got one more marking period to make it work. If you want to apply to college, you need to start doing so in January, after your next report card comes out. And if you don't bring your grades up, you won't be able to play—"

"I know. I'm sorry if I let you down, Dad," I said. "It's just hard up there."

He rambled on about how hard it was to live away from home and be independent, but I knew those things weren't my problem. In my head, I began to blame the whole thing on Sam and the Statesmen, but it wasn't their fault. They hadn't really done anything to keep me from studying, unless you counted that one night.

"I'm not going to lie to you and say I'm going to try to do better next marking period," I said.

He was shocked. "You're not?"

"No, I'm not going to say I'm going to try to do better anymore."

"What are you going to say, then, young lady?"

"I'm just going to do better. Period." Right then, I decided I was going to fix everything: my grades, my attitude, and the Statesmen's plot to get me thrown out of school. Somehow, just as Justin said, I would make everything okay.

He leaned over and patted me on the back. "Now, that sounds like the best idea I've ever heard."

"Thanks."

"Oh, and I forgot to mention one last thing."

"What's that?"

"I signed you up for the SATs—second Saturday in December."

I looked out at the long road ahead and nodded.

Chapter 12

I put my game face on first thing Monday morning. I was determined to accomplish two things by the end of the week: get an A on my upcoming quiz in Trig and find out what Sam Barrett had lied about. But I wasn't going to let this second goal distract me from focusing on the first. Doing better at Hazelton was, after all, my last real shot at college.

I came up with a plan for taking Barrett by surprise. I conveniently picked up his sweatshirt that he had left on one of the gym benches, then waited for him outside after practice, assuming he would come back to look for it and, I hoped, return alone.

I stood at the end of the hall next to a faculty bathroom, which was always unlocked so I could use it after workouts. I heard him approaching, so I hung the sweatshirt on the doorknob, stepped inside the bathroom, and waited. When his footsteps were close, I swung the door open quickly and pulled him inside, using the arm of the sweatshirt.

"What the—?"

I slammed the door and flicked on the light, holding the sweatshirt hostage in my arms. "Sam, thanks for coming. Have a seat," I said, pointing to the toilet.

He looked surprised, but at the same time sort of happy. He smiled at me. "Nah, I'm good," he said, and remained standing. "What's going on, Dresden? I thought you didn't want to talk to me."

"Frankly, I don't, but my curiosity got the best of me. That's why I arranged this little meeting."

He looked around at the small, green-tiled bathroom. "Nice choice of venue."

"Thanks. So spill it," I said, crossing my arms.

"Spill what?" he asked.

"You said you would tell me the whole truth."

"I believe I said I would tell you the whole truth if you agreed to let me tutor you in Trig," he said.

"I appreciate the offer and the good will, and I understand you feel bad about drugging me and all, but I don't need a tutor," I said. "So I'll just take the truth."

He squinted and looked up, thinking. "Nah," he said, "I still want to do the tutoring thing. It's the least I can do."

"Truth, Barrett," I said, cracking my knuckles.

"Tutor," he said in a teasing tone.

"Truth." I was getting annoyed.

"You are a feisty one, aren't you?" he asked with a smirk.

"Why do you care so much about tutoring me? Honestly, if this is a part of the great Statesmen's plot to get me thrown out of here, you're making it way too obvious."

"I told you I'm not doing that stuff anymore," he said as he stared down at his shoes, like a little boy put in the corner for a time-out.

"So you quit the group?"

"I can't quit. They'd do worse to me than they want to do to you. No one has ever quit before. So I've just quit mentally."

"Well, aren't you the noble soldier?" I said.

"Listen, if I tell you the truth, then will you at least consider letting me help you with Trig?"

"Okay, I'll consider it," I lied.

He looked around. "Could we at least walk outside?"

"Aren't you afraid to be seen with me?"

"No. People will just assume I'm setting you up," he said with a shrug.

"Right, including me."

"Where's the trust, Dresden?" He held up his arms like a suspect looking to get patted down.

"Uh, it was lost somewhere between the gym and your dorm room."

He opened the door. "Shall we?" he said, gesturing and allowing me to go first. *All right, so maybe walking with him won't hurt anything.* Besides, it was hard to resist his gorgeous stupid face smiling at me and his perfect hands holding open a door for me.

Man, I miss Justin. This being-mean-to-Sam thing would be so much easier if I still had a boyfriend around to keep my hormones in check. I'll just try to picture Sam as what he is—an ugly pig.

It was cold that day, so there weren't many people around when we got outside. The leaves were gone from the trees, and I quickly zipped up my fleece jacket, bracing myself for the wind.

He took off his knit hat. "You want this?"

I pushed his hand away. "No, stop trying to be nice to me," I said. "I don't like you, remember?" *Yeah, that'll show him.*

He put the hat back on. "Right, sorry."

I decided to head back toward the Richards house, since it was my territory. "Whenever you're ready to talk, I'm all ears," I said.

"Okay," he said with a sigh. "So the truth is I do know who

drugged you."

I knew it! "Okay, so who was it?"

"My brother Ben. He slipped something into your soda can while you weren't looking," he said. *Wow, he's throwing his own twin brother under the bus.*

I remembered talking to Ben by the refreshment table that night. *That jerk!* He was acting like he was Mr. Nice Guy, and I even thought he might actually be hitting on me. I was such a fool. But all I said was, "Why?"

"Statesmen's orders."

"But I thought you were their leader," I said, rubbing my temple.

"I am," he said quickly.

"So whose idea was drugging me?"

"Tuttle's."

"Didn't he have to okay it with you?"

"I wasn't at that meeting. I pretended I had to see one of my teachers, so the decision was made by the second-in-command."

"And that is?"

"My brother."

"Okay, but you still knew about it, right?" I said.

"Not until that night," he said, sounding sincere.

"And you didn't try to stop it, did you?"

"By the time I found out, Ben had already slipped the stuff into your drink." He stopped walking and turned. Looking me in the eye, he said, "I'm really sorry, Dresden. As soon as I knew, I followed you and made sure I got you out of there so they couldn't complete the rest of their plan."

I had to know. "What was the rest of the plan?"

"They were going to take some, uh, pictures of you."

"Doing what?!"

"Let's just say they wouldn't make your parents too proud."

I was fuming. "And then what?" I said. "They were going to show them to the school officials, or to students?"

"Anybody and everybody."

This was definitely the last conversation I wanted to have with Sam Barrett. But I had to hear the rest. "Still listening," I said coldly.

"Anyway, once he drugged you, I snuck out and followed you into the hall. After you passed out, I carried you back to my dorm. I sent a text to the guys saying you had managed to stumble back to Dr. Rich's, and they called off the rest of the plan."

We were standing in front of my Hazleton house. A few guys were looking at us from a distance. "Well, you're quite the hero," I said, my arms crossed tightly across my chest. I couldn't get out of my head the image of him carrying me.

"I'm not asking for your gratitude here, Dresden. I'm apologizing for being involved at all. I know you probably think I'm a jackass, but I truly am sorry, and if there is anything I can do for you—"

I put up my hand. "Anything you can do for me? Anything you can do?" I said, raising my voice. I stepped up toward the door. "What you can do, Sam Barrett, is leave me alone." I climbed the first step to the house, and then turned back to him. "And one more thing. Tell your friends to watch out. Because if they ever face me on the ball field, first chance I get, I'll take out their kneecaps." I slammed the door in his face.

For the rest of that night, I occupied myself with homework, trying with every ounce of my brain to understand Trig. I didn't really want to think about what Sam had told me. I decided it would just be easier for me to be angry with him than to try to decide if he was legitimately sorry or if he was just trying to trick me. A person could lose her mind trying to figure all this out. I was only seventeen, after all. My brain was going to explode if this craziness kept up. *Focus on school. Focus on getting stronger for baseball season. Just focus.*

After our conversation, whenever I saw Sam in the hallways between classes, something had changed, or switched. He looked at me, but I avoided him. He tried his hardest to make eye contact with me, and I tried my best to look anywhere but at him.

It was so hard. Part of me needed someone to trust. And I wasn't sure how much longer I could play the loner.

Chapter 13

That Friday, I truly tried to focus, but my brain let me down. On my first math quiz after the Thanksgiving break, I got a D. The following Friday, my brain failed me again, and I only made a C.

The next day was the SATs. I had worked through some test prep books that Mrs. Richards had lent me, but I figured that, by this point in my high school career, I knew what I knew and there wasn't much I could do about it.

That Saturday, I sat in the Hazelton auditorium with about fifty other kids and finally took the SATs. They actually weren't that bad, but I felt relieved when they were over. I was proud of myself for not running out on it, and for tackling something I had feared.

There were now two weeks until Christmas break. That meant two more math quizzes and one more test to try to make up for my previous C and D.

The Monday after the SATs, I was in the bubble working with the pitching coach. He had driven me over early on the short bus so we could get some time in before the guys came over for batting practice.

It was so cool to be on that enormous domed baseball field. You felt like you were outside on a warm spring day, even when the weather outside was cold. I liked standing on the mound and looking up at the rafters and seeing the bright white light that made the entire bubble glow.

Coach Madison and I first worked together on some stretching exercises, and then I threw a few. We talked a lot about control and how to place the ball right where you wanted it to go. Eventually, Coach Davenport arrived with the guys. He approached Madison and asked, "Hey, Tommy, how about we do some real batting practice against some real pitching today?"

"What'd you have in mind?" said Madison.

"I got ten guys here for batting practice, and you got a pitcher, right?"

"I do," he said, nodding in my direction. "What do you think, Taylor?"

"Fine by me," I said. "I haven't seen any real batters since last summer." In fact, I was excited to try out on actual batters some of what Madison had been teaching me.

"Okay, Davenport, we'll be out there in ten."

I felt myself kick into pre-game mode. I walked over to the water fountain and wet my hands. I ran them through my hair, pushing it away from my face before slamming my hat down to hold it back. I didn't have anything to tie my hair back with, so I would have to work with it down today.

Each guy would get three warm-up pitches and then three real pitches before rotating. A couple guys were in the field just to shag the balls and toss them back in. Most of the guys were sophomores and juniors, but I recognized a few seniors.

First guy up was Chan, a sophomore. I lobbed him three balls, and he connected nicely, sending each one to deep center field.

"Okay, Dresden, give him some heat," Coach Madison said

from the first-base side.

I smiled at him and nodded. I wound up and threw. *Thwap!* I heard the ball slam into the catcher's glove. I loved the sound of that echo. The boys in the dugout hooted. "Woo, Chan, I felt the breeze on that swing. She got you on that one. Woo!" This was going to be fun.

Chan missed the next one and didn't even swing at the third. He hung his head and went off to talk to the batting coach.

The next two batters went down just as easily. Maybe this prep-school stuff wasn't going to be any more challenging than my old high school team or my summer league. *Not again,* I thought. *I need a challenge.*

And then, there he was, standing on the left side of the plate, digging his cleats into the batter's box and taking a few practice swings—the captain of the team himself, Sam Barrett. A lump formed in my throat, and I looked out into center field for a moment. I tucked my glove between my legs, took off my cap, and forced my hair back with my fingers before putting my cap back on. Then I put my glove back on and played with the ball, repeatedly slamming it into my glove. Coach Madison had told me to save my curve ball. And I was glad I did, 'cause I felt like I was going to need it now.

"All right, Dresden, three warm-ups!" Coach Davenport yelled from behind the plate.

I gave Sam his three meatballs. He smacked two deep into right field and lined one up the middle.

Now the game was on. I so badly wanted to make him swing and miss. Unable to control myself, I wound up and delivered my curve ball first. Sure enough, the ball flew past his swinging bat. He backed out of the box and looked right at me. Pointing his bat at me, he tapped his cap with it, smiling—you know, the kind of smile that said, "Oh good, a challenge," as if he, too, had been waiting for just this moment.

But then he totally surprised me—he walked around to the other side of the plate. *He's a switch hitter. Is righty his better side? I guess I'll find out.* He stepped into the box and dug his feet into the dirt. One fastball coming up.

I heard the bat make contact with the ball. *Ting!* The ball sailed over second base and rolled into center field—a base hit in any league. *Barrett got a hit off me!*

I stood on the mound and returned his smile. As much as it hurt to give up a hit to someone trying to ruin my life, I was thankful I had met my match. It was right to come to this school. I was going to get the challenge I needed.

Of course, now I had to beat him on this last pitch. I took my glove off and cracked my knuckles.

"Uh-oh, Barrett, now you've pissed her off," Madison said with a laugh. "Get the gun on this next one, Davenport!" he said, still laughing.

On the last one, Barrett stood frozen. It was in the catcher's glove before he even saw it.

"Seventy-nine!" Davenport yelled.

Barrett walked back to the dugout, and I danced—well, on the inside anyway.

After practice, we rode back to school on the bus. My arm was sore from all the pitching, and I might have overextended myself on that last fastball to Barrett, but I decided the pain was well worth the victory. Madison had given me an ice pack and warned me against throwing my arm out—something people were always cautioning me about. I envisioned my arm one day suddenly detaching from my body and heading straight for the batter, and then me tossing my used arm into the nearest garbage can. "You see, I told her she'd throw her arm out," the coach would say.

After we returned to school, I got off the bus and walked up the blacktop path toward the Richardses. I was exhausted, but I still needed to study.

My cell phone buzzed inside my jacket. "Unknown Caller." I answered anyway.

"Need a study partner yet?" the voice asked.

"Barrett, how did you get my number?"

In his most innocent voice, he said, "I'll tell you over Trig."

"When are you going to quit with this?" I said.

"When are *you* going to quit?" he asked.

"I don't quit—anything," I said boldly.

"That's obvious. Did you enjoy embarrassing me on the field today?"

I smiled and said, "You did hit *one* of them."

"Big deal."

"It *is* a big deal. You obviously don't realize how good I am. You know the last time a guy got a decent hit off me?" *Stop flirting, Taylor. You hate him, remember?*

"I have a feeling you're going to tell me."

"My sophomore year," I said.

"You *are* good. I guess I should be proud of my one little hit then, huh?"

"You should be." *Stop it. Stop being nice!*

"Okay, so get cleaned up, eat, and I'll meet you at the library at 7:30," he said.

"Bye, Sam," I sang, hanging up. I needed to stop enjoying talking to him. But it was so hard not to be flattered by the attention. He looked so good staring me down from that batter's box today. And he was good. It didn't bother me that he was obviously one of the best ballplayers I had ever come up against.

I then wondered if the big jerk would really be at the library waiting for me when he said he would. Would one tutoring session hurt? I needed to get a good grade on this next quiz. After all, it had been over a month since the dance, and he hadn't tried anything. Maybe I could trust him. I just wished I had proof he wasn't a big two-faced liar.

I couldn't sit still that night. After I finished my History paper, I couldn't bring myself to do my Trig homework. I kept thinking of Sam Barrett sitting in the library waiting for me. I could always just wander over there and see if he was really there, and if he wasn't, I could go ahead and finish my homework in the library.

I knew I had to get out of my bedroom, or I was never going to relax. My stubborn will to ignore him was slowly losing out. Something about him staring from under that batter's helmet had gotten to me.

Before I knew it, I was standing in front of the mirror, brushing my hair and putting on clear lip gloss before grabbing my book bag and heading over to the library. I walked down the aisles to the spot where I ran into him last time. I sat down at the desk and tried to study, but really, I was just waiting to see if he would show. I heard a rustle of books and a jacket unzipping in the cubicle opposite me. I couldn't see anyone, and no one could see me. I began to hear whispers.

"Hey, Captain," said the first voice. "You studying?"

"Yeah, I have a Calc test this week. Why? What's up?" Sam whispered back.

"We had our weekly council meeting tonight and you didn't show." Now I recognized the other voice as Tuttle's, who continued, "Thought you might be sick or something. "

"Nah, just studying. Sorry, man. I totally lost track of time."

"No prob, but we need to fill you in on Plan B."

"Plan B?"

Tuttle's voice got quieter. "Yeah, you know, getting rid of enemy number two."

Barrett sighed. "You guys haven't given up on that yet?"

"No, man, we've got to get back at this place for what they did to McCarthy. Besides, this whole thing was *your* idea in the first place. You know, the guys have been talking, and we're not feeling the love from you lately. You miss meetings, and when you're there, you never say anything."

"Yeah, sorry. Just got a lot of stuff going on these days."

"What? With your parents again?"

"I don't really want to talk about it," said Sam. "If you want, I'll meet you guys tomorrow."

"Cool. Usual place?"

"You got it."

There was a quick slap of hands, and then nothing else. I think I had my proof. He *was* trying to help. I tossed a note over the desktop: "What's the difference between sine and cosine? –A Trig Failure".

He stood up at his desk and leaned over the top of the cubicle. "Hi," he whispered, giving me the biggest smile.

I couldn't do anything else but smile back. At that moment, I asked myself, *What are you getting yourself into, Taylor?*

Sam pulled his chair around to my cubicle and began teaching me everything he knew about Trig. Not only was he really smart, but he was surprisingly patient, even when I asked him to repeat every other thing.

After about an hour and a half, my brain was worn out. I wasn't sure if it was from the studying or from the mental stress of sitting next to him for so long.

True, my guard was down, but I was pretty sure I could trust him.

Now, it was more about not letting him know how attracted to him I was. Yes, he had found it in himself to protect me from his stupid Statesmen friends, but I couldn't assume that meant he was also interested in me. I let out a big yawn.

"You're beat, aren't you?" he said.

"No, I can keep going if you want," I said, trying to suppress another yawn.

He laughed quietly. "I think we've done enough for one night."

I nodded. "Honestly, I think I stopped listening twenty minutes ago. I'm sorry."

"It's okay. Same time tomorrow?"

"If you have the time . . . I mean, I'm sure you have studying of your own to do," I said, feeling a little guilty he'd be spending so much time on me.

"It's no problem." He started packing his book bag. "So tomorrow, then? Same place?"

I got up and slung my bag over my shoulder. "Okay. I really appreciate it."

"You know I wanted to do this weeks ago."

"I guess."

"So, just one question," he said as he got up from the desk.

"What?" I asked as we walked slowly, side by side, toward the exit.

"Why did you finally decide to trust me?"

I felt guilty about my earlier eavesdropping, so I said, "I figured I'd just take a leap of faith."

"And if it proves to be a bad leap?"

"Then you'd better make sure you're wearing a cup next time you bat against me," I said, opening the door for him.

He raised an eyebrow and smiled.

Chapter 14

I spent the next few nights in the library sitting shoulder-to-shoulder with Sam Barrett. It was the best time I ever had studying. After we finished one session, he walked me back to the Richards house. It took a good ten minutes, and I enjoyed every moment with him in the dark.

"So, I've been meaning to ask, why were you guys so upset about what happened to Mike McCarthy?" I turned to him.

"You don't know?" he asked, looking surprised.

"I know he was expelled for missing curfew, but what's that got to do with me and Gabby?"

"Well, he *is* kind of the reason you're here," Sam said.

"What do you mean?"

"Well, the abridged version is that Mike, who was in my class, was rumored to be having an affair with one of the teachers, Ms. Abernathy."

"Ms. Abernathy? Oh, the one suing the school?" I said.

"Yeah. They fired her last spring, which is when they threw Mike out of school."

"So what does that have to do with me?" I said.

"Well, Abernathy sued the school, saying they were discriminating against women, and that they were looking for any reason to get rid of her. There was a lot of bad press. A lot of the alumni stopped making donations," said Sam. "You and

Gabby and Kwan were supposed to make Hazelton look good again. You know, bring in some girls, prove the school's not sexist. You get the picture."

"So Gabby was right."

"About what?"

"She figured our being offered scholarships had something to do with money."

He nodded. "You have no idea how much some of the alumni donate to this place."

"And that's why they told Gabby she could come back, even after they thought she was stealing—because they were afraid to lose more donations," I concluded.

"Exactly."

"I guess this should piss me off, huh?" I said.

"I don't know. Does it?"

"I'm not sure, to be honest. I guess they're using me for good press, but I'm kind of using them, too."

"You are?"

"Yeah. Well, I'm using them for baseball," I said. "And my dad is using them to help get me into college."

"Didn't college recruiters scout your old school?"

"Yeah, sometimes. They saw me pitch and were thrilled to talk to me, but then they saw my grades. My dad thinks if I can just get decent grades here, scouts will assume I must be smart."

"You didn't have to take the entrance exam, did you?" he asked, smiling and shaking his head.

"Nope. Neither did Gabby. The headmaster said our grades were fine."

Sam laughed. "They do whatever they want here. They just change the rules whenever it suits them."

"So that's why the Statesmen were angry about Mike?" I asked, kicking at a rock on the walkway.

"Yeah. Mike was a good guy, and the school didn't buy his side of the story."

"Do you think he had an affair with the teacher?"

"Nah. She'd never have done that," Sam said, shaking his head. "She was a beautiful woman, but she was too responsible to do something like that."

"Did you ever ask Mike about it?" I asked.

"Yeah. He said all he did was give her a ride to her car one night when it was raining downtown. He was really into her, but nothing happened."

"But somebody saw them together?" I said.

"And turned it into a big scandal," he said.

"A lot of games go on around here."

"And you've only been here a few months."

"Speaking of rules and games, what about Plan B?"

Sam didn't say anything at first. He had a look of shame in his eyes. "I'm sorry about all this, Taylor. I hate being a part of this stupidity. I—"

"Barrett, relax. It's okay. Just tell me what I should watch out for," I said.

"Promise you won't be mad?" he asked, stopping and turning toward me.

"Spill it, Barrett," I said, as I stopped walking.

"They figured since your grades were bad, they'd just make sure they stayed that way, so you'd flunk out."

I crossed my arms. "And you're supposed to be helping me fail Trig?"

"That's what they think, but I guess the joke will be on them when you ace your quiz tomorrow."

"I hope you're right," I said, heading again toward the Richards house.

"You know this stuff, Dresden. You'll be fine." He skipped forward to catch up with me.

"I guess the fact that I'm a pitcher pisses Tuttle off even more, huh?"

"Doesn't help."

"I just gotta know one more thing," I said.

"What's that?"

"Why did you decide to go against them and help me?"

He breathed out, looked up at the Richardses' house, and shook his head. "I don't know exactly. One day, I looked at you in the gym, and you were trying so hard to look tough and—"

"You pitied me," I said.

"No, it wasn't pity," he said. "I just realized you were a human being, with feelings. There's something about you, Dresden, that's . . . that's got to me, I guess."

There was a warm glow coming from the dining room window of the Richards house. I wished we had farther to walk so the conversation wouldn't have to end. I was getting spoiled having someone to talk to the last few nights, not to mention just being able to look at him two hours every night.

Watching his mouth as he talked about Trig and watching, meticulously, his every movement was starting to get to me. I looked at him in the glow of the house lights and wondered if he had any flaws. His face was perfect. His hair was perfect. His smell was perfect. And I stood there, the tall, skinny girl with stringy hair, wondering why he was standing in this beautiful light with someone as plain as me. "Well," I said, looking toward the front door, "I should go."

He nodded. "Goodnight."

"Thanks for helping me."

"The least I could do."

And then I remembered he was just doing charity work to atone for his past wrongdoing.

"Just the same, thank you," I said.

Chapter 15

Not only did I pass the next day's quiz, but I got an A-. I stared at the ninety-one written at the top of my paper and double-checked to make sure it was mine. Then I did a small, girly jump of joy.

"Nice job, Miss Dresden," Mr. Moesch said as I glided out the door.

"Thanks." I couldn't wait to tell Sam.

But I knew I couldn't really talk to him in school, so I ducked into the women's room to send him a text message. I couldn't wait until nightfall to share the news.

I wrote: "I got an A-!"

I waited a minute, but got no response. Maybe his phone was off. We weren't supposed to have them on in school, but we followed that rule as strictly as adults follow the no-cell phone law while driving. *Oh, well, I'll have to tell him later.*

Unfortunately, later never happened, at least that day. He wasn't working out after school, and though he hadn't told me to meet him in the library that night, I went anyway, only to find our usual corner empty. He didn't call or text. I tried to rationalize his silence. He had agreed to tutor me, but maybe that was all.

Yet, for some reason, I felt like he was more than my tutor. I guess I had fooled myself into thinking we were becoming friends. It hurt not to have anyone to share my victory with, so I shared it with Dr. Rich that night.

I found him in his den reading a magazine and having his after-dinner coffee. "Got an A on my Trig quiz!" I proclaimed.

He looked up from his magazine and over his reading glasses. "Well, that's good news."

I leaned against the doorway. "It is, isn't it?"

"And your SAT scores are here if you feel like opening this," he said, pointing to an envelope on his desk.

I wasn't sure if I wanted to ruin my good quiz grade with some low SAT scores. "Hmm, I have to think about that."

"Eh, go ahead, open it. Maybe it's your lucky day."

I picked up the envelope and started to tear it open. "What's a good score, Dr. Rich?" I said.

"Depends on what you mean by 'good.'"

"You know, like, good enough to get into a halfway decent college with a good baseball program."

"I'd say anything over seventeen hundred would suffice."

I slowly unfolded the letter. I glanced all over the paper until I found the total—1840. I looked at Dr. Rich and smiled. "I've got to call my dad!" I said, and happily ran up to my room.

The next few days, I waited in vain to hear back from Sam. I did see him in the hall a few times, but he was always surrounded by the evil Statesmen. It was as if any time I came near him, they appeared out of nowhere and swarmed him. I couldn't even catch a simple glance.

Friday was the beginning of Christmas break, and when my dad and brother pulled up in front of the Richards house to pick me up, I looked around campus before getting in the car, waiting to see if perhaps Sam would come out of the bushes and wish me a merry Christmas.

All I heard was the sound of car doors slamming as other parents picked up their kids. Sam Barrett was nowhere to be seen or heard. Maybe I had misinterpreted the whole situation. I wanted to be angry at him for ignoring me, but all I could bring myself to feel was disappointment in not getting to talk with him before the long break.

"Hey, 1840," my dad said as I got into the car.

"Hi, Dad."

"All right, let's blow this brain barn!" he said, chuckling.

Over the break, I found it difficult to relax. I had nightmares about the Statesmen ruining my life, nightmares about flunking out, and nightmares about being unable to throw strikes at spring tryouts.

I did have a few good dreams about Sam Barrett, but they were really bad dreams because I knew they would never become reality. I checked my phone and e-mail daily, but just like the snow I was hoping for on Christmas Eve, no Sam communication came.

There was a different sort of storm brewing that evening.

On Christmas Eve at my house, my dad, my brothers, and I usually sat around the family room watching whatever movie we could all agree on. But my older brother, Brian, hadn't come home this year. It was his first year out of college, and he was working at a sales job in Arizona and didn't have enough time or money to get home for the holiday. So it was just the three of us.

And for the first time ever, my dad, without warning, turned the TV off in the middle of the movie.

"Hey, Pops, what gives?" Dan said.

It was weird for my dad to turn the TV off, even if there was nothing good on. Dad was famous for falling asleep at night with the television on and then waking up in front of it in the morning and catching the news without missing a beat.

Sometimes, I thought he used it to keep from thinking about how lonely he truly was. He wasn't an old man, after all. He was only forty-five. I knew most kids viewed their parents as old, but the funny thing was, the older I got, the younger he seemed to me.

"What's up, Dad?" I said. "Something wrong?" *Maybe he knows what's happening to me at school.*

"Yeah, there is. Well, no, that's the wrong way of saying it. Nothing's really wrong, exactly," he said. "I just need to talk to you guys about something I should've told you a few months ago."

"Are you pregnant?" Dan said.

Dad laughed lightly. "No, are you?" he said to Dan.

They both turned my way. "Don't look at me," I said with a shrug.

We all laughed. "Seriously, give me a minute to explain, then barrage me with questions, or get mad or whatever," Dad said.

"Why would we be mad at you?" I asked. *What's going on?*

"He's addicted to crack!" Dan said.

"Enough jokes, Dan," I said, trying not to laugh with him.

"Okay," said Dad, "so a few months ago—I guess it was mid-August or so—I got a call from a man named Darren Orville."

"Who's that?" I asked.

"He's your mother's fiancé, actually."

For once, Dan was speechless. So was I.

"That's the reaction I thought I'd get. Anyway, he called to give me some news about your mother that I guess he thought we deserved to know."

"Is she okay?" I surprised myself with my sudden concern.

"She's fine now. Well, as fine as can be expected, I suppose."

"What happened?" I asked.

"Long story short, your mom's been suffering from depression for most of her life. I didn't really understand that when we were married. I thought, you know, women are moody. But I guess it's more than that," he said. "Years after she left, she called me and told me she was in treatment and taking medication to help. I thought that was that. But after speaking with Darren, I realized it was much more serious than I was aware of."

"Serious how?" I said.

He rubbed his chin and then massaged his brow. "She took a lot more pills than she was supposed to. She tried to kill herself."

Over the years, I had thought of my mom not so much as a deserter of our family, but as a flake. I always pictured her as selfish and immature and too spacey to be tied down to one man and one family. I'm not sure why I had that image of her. I guess it was more comforting to think she was flaky than that she hated all of us. But it never once crossed my mind that she was mentally ill.

Dan spoke before I could. "So, she's nuts," he said, seemingly comfortable simply writing her off as a nut bag and moving on with his life.

"No, Dan, she's not nuts. Depression is really complicated. I'm just now learning about it myself, and to be honest, it has helped me forgive her a little for leaving."

"Depressed or not, Dad, she left," Dan said. "In my book, that made her a bitch. Now she's just a crazy bitch."

"Daniel, I never want to hear you speak that way about your mother ever again," said Dad. "I know she left when you were very young, but I won't tolerate that language about the woman who gave birth to you."

Dan backed off and looked out the window at the streetlights.

I couldn't figure out how I felt. Did this news make it better—knowing she left because of depression? *And what is that really? Is that a reason to ditch your family?* "Dad?" I said quietly.

"Yes, honey?"

"She's not dead, is she?"

"No, honey. Darren found her in time and rushed her to the emergency room. She's been at a treatment center since the summer. And Darren called last week to tell me she's feeling much better."

Dan got up and paced around before parking himself by the kitchen doorway. "So what's the point of telling us all this now?" he asked, not trying to hide how upset he was.

"As a part of her therapy, she has to deal with her past and make apologies to people she wronged as a result of her depression," said Dad. "Darren says she's been carrying around a lot of guilt about what she did to you guys, and I guess she wants a chance to explain herself."

"What, so we can tell her we forgive her so she'll feel better about herself?!" Dan yelled.

"Dan, relax. You don't have to if you don't want to."

"Well, good, 'cause I don't want to."

Until then, I'd never realized how angry Dan was about

Mom. He was only two years old when she left. He had absolutely no memory of her, but he seemed the angriest of us all.

"Listen, it's up to you guys. If you want to talk with her, it'd be on your terms. But no pressure to do anything."

"Where does she even live?" I asked.

"Right outside of Philadelphia."

She's that close? Has she been that close all these years? Just one state over?

"Really?" I said.

"You're not considering talking to her, are you, T?" Dan asked.

"I don't know. Maybe."

"You could do it face to face or over the phone," Dad said. "Whatever you want, honey. Or not at all."

"Have you talked to her, Dad?" I said.

"Yeah, about a week ago," he said. "Just on the phone. We talked for over an hour. I told her about you attending Hazelton and how well Dan's doing in school. She was really interested in what you guys are doing, and I have to admit"— he paused and rubbed his head again—"it was nice. She seems different somehow. Better than before."

I was getting more curious about her. When I thought she was thousands of miles away in Flakeland, I hadn't cared about her. But she was only an hour away. And the thought that she might have died before I had a chance to talk to her kind of made me want to do it before it was too late.

What if she had died and I hadn't talked to her? What if I don't get a second chance? Maybe that's what I should be learning from all this crap at Hazelton—to take a chance when I'm given one. Just as Hazelton was my last chance to get into a good college, maybe this was my last chance to make peace with my mother.

"I'll think about it," I said finally.

Chapter 16

When school resumed after the winter break, I felt happy. I was eager to maintain my new studious attitude all the way through the marking period.

I was still thinking about whether or not to talk to my mother. Dad assured me there was no rush and to call him if and when I felt up to it. I wanted to do it. I just wasn't sure of exactly when. Dad kept reminding me that at the end of the marking period, we would have to start applying to colleges. I also realized that in a month, baseball tryouts would start. Everything was happening at once—and too quickly.

That Monday, I did not see Sam Barrett anywhere. He was not in the halls, not in the café, and not in the gym. His brother, Ben, was there, but not Sam. Guessing he must be sick, I figured I would see him around the next day. But Tuesday came and went, as did Wednesday and Thursday, and still there was no sign of Sam Barrett. I desperately wished I could ask someone where he was, but nobody spoke to me other than the teachers and coaches.

In the bubble that Friday afternoon, we had another round of batting practice. I was taking turns pitching with a sophomore, Todd Leary.

"Hey, Coach Madison," I said casually while warming up in the bullpen. "Is that one guy who got a hit off me last time here today?" I knew he wasn't on the bus earlier, but I asked just the same.

"Oh yeah, uh, Barrett, right?"

"Yeah, I think that was his name," I said. "I'd like to face him again and see if I can strike him out this time."

"Hey, Davenport, is Barrett practicing today?" he yelled toward the dugout.

"No, he's sick—mono or something."

Coach shrugged. "Don't worry, we'll find you a challenge."

Mono? Justin's cousin had had mono last year and he was out of school for almost two months. I hoped Coach was wrong. Two months without seeing him?

I needed to stop obsessing. He didn't like me anyway. He was just my tutor. *Get a grip—now! Focus on school and pitching. Stop being a girl.* I was angry, though, at the thought of being on my own against the Statesmen turds who wanted me out.

"Okay, Dresden, get in there for a while," said Coach.

Three batters quickly came and went. The fourth guy up was Grossman. He was taller than most of the guys I had faced. *Why did that name ring a bell?*

And then it hit me. He was on the basketball team, too. He had to be Gabby's Grossman. He was the one who had given her the key and gotten her into trouble.

Suddenly, my strike zone changed. I was thinking about brushback pitches—maybe one to the knees, or possibly one to the wrist. Nothing like a crack on the wrist to teach a big prep-school jerk a lesson. I just couldn't resist. I sent a fastball inside, plunking him right on the wrist.

He winced and jumped back, dropping the bat.

"Oh, sorry," I said, trying to act as if I cared.

He glared at me and held his wrist. By the look on his face,

I could tell he knew I'd done it on purpose. I just pulled my hat down over my eyes and stepped off the mound.

Coach Davenport came over to Grossman. "It's nothing," Coach told him. "You'll live. Just go put some ice on it so it doesn't swell up on you."

"Dresden, you can't get so wild," said Madison, walking over to me. "Focus on your zone and hit the spot you want to hit!"

I just smiled.

"Is something funny?"

"No."

"No, but you were smiling." He looked over toward Grossman, who was still giving me a nasty stare. "You hit him on purpose, didn't you?"

"No, I didn't," I said, avoiding the coach's eyes.

He got in front of me and stared right at me. "You're a really bad liar," he said.

I shrugged. "He had it coming, Coach."

He smiled and crossed his arms across his chest. "Just tell me one thing, Dresden."

"What?"

"Were you aiming for his wrist?"

"Damn right I was," I said, and then popped a bubble with my gum.

"Well, at least your command is improving." He sighed and tossed the ball back to me. "Keep personal agendas off the field. Stuff like that will ruin you."

"Sorry, Coach."

"Uh-huh. Just pitch, Dresden."

The strange thing was, I thought getting a little revenge for Gabby would make me feel good, but it didn't. As I watched Grossman walk over and grab an ice bag from the cooler, I didn't feel the slightest bit better.

There was still no sign of Sam Barrett the following week. First thing Tuesday morning, I received a message to report to the headmaster's office during my study period. I was hoping it wasn't about my grades, because I was trying my best to keep them up. Maybe it was about baseball.

In the back of my mind, though, I hoped it had something to do with Sam's absence. Of course, that would be pointless and stupid. How would the headmaster know I had a huge crush on Sam Barrett?

When I walked into his office, Dr. Colton said, "Miss Dresden, have a seat."

I sat down.

"I wanted to ask you a few questions about your time here so far at Hazelton. Are you enjoying our school?"

"Yes, sir, it's very nice. The teachers and coaches are very helpful," I said.

"And the students?"

"They're fine," I lied.

"They're treating you well, then?"

"Is there some sort of problem?" I asked.

"Well, it seems Miss Kwan has decided to leave school. Her parents phoned me this morning and informed me that she did not feel at ease here," he said. "She said some of the students were making her uncomfortable."

They got Kwan. Now it's just me. I didn't know what to say. Should I tell him about the Statesmen? Did he know about them? I dropped a hint. "Did she say anything about any of the guys bullying her?"

"Bullying?" he asked, confused. "She didn't mention anything like that, Miss Dresden. Do you think bullying occurs here at Hazelton?"

"I don't know. Maybe," I said taking a shot that, unlike Dr. Rich, maybe he would believe me.

"The students at Hazelton adhere to a very strict honor code, and I can assure you that nothing like that happens at our school," he stated with a sense of certainty.

Well, he was clueless, and obviously not ready to believe what was really going on, so I changed the subject. "Maybe she just wasn't used to all the boys. I'm used to being around boys, 'cause of the baseball thing and all. Maybe she just missed her girl friends."

"Perhaps you're right. She's a bit younger than you, too. I'm just concerned that you're our only girl left," said Dr. Colton. "Will this be a problem for you, Miss Dresden?"

"Not at all, sir."

As I rose to leave, I thought, *Wow. Now I've got to put my game face on and keep it.*

I stopped myself at the door. "Dr. Colton?"

"Yes, Miss Dresden?"

"Do you happen to know what's wrong with Sam Barrett? I only ask because he was tutoring me in Trig and I haven't seen him since before Christmas break."

"Mr. Barrett returns on Monday," he said tersely.

"Thank you, sir."

That night, during dinner at the Richards house, the

doorbell rang. That had never happened during a meal—meals at the house were always quiet, and I usually finished first, washed my plate, and headed upstairs to give the family some time together. As Dr. Rich rose to get the door, I made my way toward the kitchen. I had a feeling something was up.

I was scraping my plate in the kitchen when Dr. Rich walked back to the table with Dr. Colton, who was holding a video tape. I found this very odd. I had never seen him in the house before tonight.

"Mrs. Richards," Dr. Colton said, shaking her hand, "you look well."

"We'll just be a minute in my office, hon," Dr. Rich said to his wife.

"Certainly," she said, continuing to feed Matthew as the two men left the dining room.

I stood in the kitchen and wondered if this was about Kwan—or me. I had to find a way to eavesdrop, but Mrs. Richards was right there. If I could make an excuse to go outside, maybe I could sneak a peek through the window at what was on that tape.

"Mrs. Richards?" I said quickly.

"Yes, dear?"

"I think I'll head over to the library for a little bit."

She nodded. "You really are motivated lately, Taylor. Good for you."

I hustled up the stairs to grab my book bag to make things look legit, then went out the front door. Luckily, it was dark outside, so I could easily hide between the bushes and the house. I crept along the side of the house and positioned myself underneath what I was pretty sure was the office window. I couldn't hear anything. *Shoot.* I had to peek. I laid my book bag down and stood on top of it. I could just see above the window ledge.

They were watching some security video footage from the school hallway, and fortunately for me, the television monitor faced in my direction. The video flickered to a start, and there was Kwan, opening her locker, with tons of notes and cards, even flowers, pouring out onto the floor.

The boys didn't have to be too inappropriate with Kwan. Just giving her attention and pretending they were all in love with her was enough to scare her off.

She was a really shy girl, probably raised by her parents to never show interest in boys. The Statesmen must have had a bunch of different boys ask her out, leave romantic notes for her, and declare their undying love. It was too much for such a quiet little girl to handle. She had stuck with it for half a year, but I guess enough was enough for Kwan.

I figured that was not the same treatment I would face. Nobody brings girls like me flowers. They assume a girl who plays baseball wouldn't go for flowers. I felt bad for Kwan, but at least I could say I'd tried to warn her.

After I saw all I needed to see, I did actually go the library. If I stayed focused on my grades, maybe I could keep from thinking about the fact that, for the Statesmen, it was two down and one to go.

Chapter 17

Sam did return that Monday, but it was like September all over again. He wouldn't look at me in the hall, making me once again the invisible woman. And he looked different somehow. He wasn't the same confident Sam Barrett. He looked tired. Instead of slapping hands with friends or strutting down the middle of the hall, he stood at his locker and let his hair fall into his eyes without pushing it back. Something was wrong.

During my study period on Monday, I went to the office for my meeting with the guidance counselor, Mr. Bass, about college applications. He was balding and short, with frameless glasses. His head kind of looked like an egg. His office had large glass windows all around it.

After about a ten-minute wait, Mr. Bass brought me into his office. He explained the parts of the college application process to me, including the transcripts and the personal essays. He told me to figure out what schools interested me, and he gave me a huge book to look at. It listed all of the schools and what programs they offered.

"Take a look at the books and the schools' websites. Apply to as many as you can," he said. "Don't be afraid to pick the schools you really think are out of your league. You never know. Any questions?"

"Nope, thanks," I said.

Later in my room, I looked at the books he gave me. The whole thing was overwhelming. I decided I would pick the schools with the best baseball programs. Mr. Bass did say you never know what could happen, and the deadline for applications was getting close. So I spent the night on college websites, typing out essays and filling out applications, trying to highlight the one thing I knew I did well—play baseball. Maybe I would get lucky.

The next week, I walked the halls on alert, figuring Plan B had to be in high gear by now. And, as it turned out, the third Friday in January was when the Statesmen made their big move.

Mr. Moesch, my Trig teacher, handed back my latest test. Ever since Sam began helping me, I had really been studying thoroughly, and I actually understood most of the material. So when I saw the failing grade written across the top of my test paper, I was shocked. *A fifty-nine?* I scanned the test quickly to find out what I had done wrong.

And that's when I noticed this wasn't even my test. It had my name at the top, but what was written below wasn't my work. It was a near-perfect imitation of my handwriting, but it wasn't mine. Someone had turned in this paper in place of my real one.

The bell rang for the end of class, and I walked out of the room like a zombie. What could I do? Would Mr. Moesch believe me if I told him it wasn't my test? How could I prove it? *Should I talk to the headmaster? He seemed concerned that I be treated fairly.*

I could feel the anger building up inside of me. I scanned the hall to see if any of the Statesmen was watching me, waiting for me to react. I kept composed. I walked to my next class just as I normally did and showed no sign that anything was bothering me.

I would find a way to fix this, I decided. I'd stay here at Hazelton and get a scholarship to a good school. I had to. I was not giving up.

After school that day, I went to see Mr. Moesch. I figured it couldn't hurt to try. Luckily, no one else was in the room. "Mr. Moesch?" I said quietly.

"Yes, Miss Dresden?"

"May I talk to you about my test?"

"Of course, have a seat," he said. "I was surprised at the low score, because you've been doing so well of late."

I explained that the test he had graded was not the test I'd completed. "I know it sounds crazy," I said, "and I'm sure you have no reason to believe what I'm telling you, but I swear to you, Mr. Moesch, that is not what I wrote." I needed to drive home my point, so I said, "You must see it, Mr. Moesch. These boys ignore me and want to mess with me. I think they're trying to be funny, or—"

"Take it easy, Miss Dresden. There's an easy way to solve this."

"There is?"

"Yes." He walked over to me and handed me a blank piece of paper. "I will put a problem on the board. If you can solve it, I will let you retake the test."

He believed me. "Thank you so much, I really appreciate—"

"Hang on now. You have to remember that it is against the

rules of the school to lie or cheat, and you have sworn to me that you are telling the truth. I am just honoring that code," he said. "Of course, if you *are* telling the truth, then one of my other students has lied, and therefore has broken the code."

I shut my mouth while he wrote a problem on the board. *God, I hope it's something I know. Please, please let me know it.* I waited as patiently as I could for him to finish writing the problem, and to move to the side so I could see it. *I know this. I got this.*

I began writing quickly. I handed him my solution and watched him look it over and then give me a nod. "Okay, tomorrow afternoon for the retake. And I will inform the headmaster that something unsettling is going on here."

I thought quickly and said, "Mr. Moesch?"

"Yes, Miss Dresden?"

"Do you think maybe you could just keep this between you and me for now?"

"Why? Someone has broken the code, and therefore certain procedures must be followed."

"I understand where you're coming from, sir, but it would really help me if the boys didn't know I was given a retake," she said. "It's better for me if they think I'm failing. Let them think they got me once and maybe they'll leave me alone. You know how boys can be, don't you? You were in school once."

I could tell by the sad look on his face that he had once been bullied, or been the victim of a prank, or the butt of someone's joke at school. He knew. He understood. "All right, Miss Dresden. If that is what you want, I will honor your request."

"Thank you, sir."

I piled up my books to leave and moved toward the door.

"And, Miss Dresden?" he said.

"Yes, sir?"

"I hear you have guts on the baseball diamond. I'm impressed it has extended to the classroom."

"Thank you, sir," I said, "and thanks again for believing me."

Dresden, one, Statesmen jerk-head losers, zero.

As I walked out of Mr. Moesch's room, I felt the anger building inside of me over what the Statesmen had done. I wanted revenge now more than ever. A crack on the wrist was just not enough. I needed to do something else, something bigger. I would have to just wait for my moment. Eventually, it would come.

Chapter 18

A few days after the math test incident, I was finishing up my afternoon workout in the gym when I heard a commotion outside the gym doors. It had snowed a few inches the night before, and I assumed it was just guys having a snowball fight.

But then something made me listen closer. Maybe it was the look on the other guys' faces in the gym. Maybe it was the low thud I heard, like the sound of a punch into someone's gut. I can't be certain, but something made me race over to the exit door and push it open.

And there they were—Tuttle, Briggs, and two other Statesmen, giving Sam Barrett a good beating. They were about twenty yards from where I stood, taking turns punching him—a blow to the stomach, one to the face—and Sam wasn't fighting back.

I was torn. I wanted to run out and help him, but that might make things worse. Then they would know he had helped me. Maybe they were beating him up because they already knew. Or maybe it was something else entirely.

My mind raced, but my feet were frozen to the ground. I didn't know what to do.

Luckily, fate stepped in and decided for me. A car pulled up along the road that ran behind the gym. I didn't know who was in the car, but its appearance was enough to scare off Tuttle and his goons. They raced around the side of the building.

Sam sat slumped against a tree. I looked behind me, then back into the gym, and saw the place had emptied out. Everyone had either run out the other side door to watch the fight or vanished so they wouldn't have to be witnesses. Nobody wanted to speak out against the Statesmen. That would be prep school suicide.

I had on just a t-shirt and shorts, but I ran outside to him. He saw me coming and raised a hand to stop me, covering his face with his other hand. "Get out of here, Dresden!" he yelled.

I stopped a few feet from him. "They're gone, Sam. Come on, let me help—"

"I said, get out of here!" He climbed to his feet, using the tree for support. With the back of his hand, he wiped blood from a cut on his already swollen lip.

"They did this to you because of me, didn't they?" I said. "Because you helped me with math."

He turned away from me and started moving slowly back up the hill toward his dorm. "You don't know what you're risking talking to me," he said through gritted teeth. "Just go back inside before you freeze to death."

I so wanted to help him, but he didn't want my help. Maybe this wasn't about me, but in my heart, I knew it was. I stood there, my arms hugging my body to shield myself from the cold. The farther away Sam Barrett got, the colder I became, and for some reason, also angrier.

The car that had driven by during the fight reappeared and pulled up near me as I crossed campus. In the car were two boys who I recognized from Chemistry. I was pretty sure the driver's name was Clifton. They both rolled down their windows. *Damn*, I thought, *more Statesmen*.

"Hey, Taylor," said the guy riding shotgun. I thought it was strange he called me by my first name.

I stopped. I was curious. "What?" I said.

"Is he okay?"

"Who?" I asked, rubbing my arms from the cold.

"Sam. Barrett. He okay?"

"Why do you care?" I was both confused and angry. Then I mumbled, "Stupid Statesmen."

"He's a good guy, you know. Looked like he got a bad beating."

I didn't know if I should trust these guys and, honestly, I didn't know if he was okay. "I don't know," I said coldly.

"Sorry I asked. Didn't mean to piss you off. Relax, Dresden. We're not *all* Statesmen, you know." He rolled up the car window and drove off.

When I got back to the Richards house, I was shaking all over, from the freezing cold weather combined with what I had just witnessed. I ran upstairs and turned on the shower as hot as it would go. I was so panicked and confused. I didn't know who *not* to trust anymore. I stood under the water, trying to get myself to stop shaking.

But the shaking continued and soon, tears began. The funny thing was that through all of this—losing Justin, losing Gabby, being drugged, knowing I was on borrowed time at school—through all of this crap, this was the first time I had cried. But my head was spinning with questions. *Why were they beating Sam up? Is it all my fault? And what about those guys in the car? Were they really trying to help Sam or are they just more guys I should watch out for? I wish this whole stupid thing would end. I wish Dad was here.*

I threw on my warmest flannel pajamas and got into bed. My hair was still wet from the shower, and it was dripping onto the pillow, but I didn't care. I called my dad on my cell.

"Hey there," said a friendly voice.

"Hi, Dad," I said softly. "Whatcha doing?"

"Just having a cup of joe and watching the news. Is it snowing up there?"

"It's stopped now, but we got a few inches."

"Just a coating here, but they're calling for more by morning." There was a bit of a pause. "Everything okay?" he asked.

I started to cry. "Just having a bad day. Sorry."

"What's the matter, honey? Did something happen?"

I tried to tell him without supplying the details. "It's lonely, and some days it's tough being the only girl here," I said. "None of the guys really talk to me. I feel like no one likes me."

"I'm sure that's not the case. I'm sure if you look around, you'll find friends you didn't even know existed."

I thought about Sam. And then I thought about that Clifton guy in the car, and what he said about not everyone being a Statesman. "Maybe," I said to my dad.

"How about this weekend, Dan and I come up and take you out to dinner? What about Saturday?"

I really wanted him to come. I needed to see someone who cared. But then, without warning, I said, "How about we arrange that meeting I was thinking about, with . . . with Mom?"

"You sure, honey? You seem like you're pretty shaken up

right now."

"Yeah, but I figure it can't possibly make me feel worse," I said. "And maybe it'll help."

"Okay, I'll give her a call and then I'll call you," said Dad. "And until then, how about you call me every night around this time and we'll talk? If you want."

"Okay, Dad, I'd like that."

"I love you, honey. I hate to think of you up there, lonely and crying."

"You know I'm not a big crier. It's just today I'm letting stuff get to me," I said.

"I know. But I feel like you went up there because of me. I feel like I forced you into this situation."

"You didn't, Dad. You were right. I needed to do this. I needed to change," I said. "And honestly, I *do* like it here. I'm learning so much from the pitching coach. Did I tell you he played in the Phillies' minor league system?"

"Only a few times," said Dad.

"And I'm finally learning things, too, Dad. I study now, for real. I don't think I'd ever have done that if I'd stayed at Evansville. I'll be fine, Dad. I swear."

"I know you will."

"Okay, I'm gonna go eat something before I crash, and then I have some studying to do."

"All right, honey," said Dad. "I love you."

"Love you, too. Thanks for listening," I said.

"Any time, sweetheart."

That night, I couldn't sleep. The images of Sam's beating

kept running through my head. I just wished I knew he was all right. Around 1 a.m., I thought it'd be a good idea to send him a text message. Maybe he would answer, and I could get a few hours of sleep. I picked up my phone and hit "Contacts." For a minute, I considered exactly what to say. I decided to keep it simple: "R u ok?"

And then came the waiting. I held the phone in my hand for about ten minutes, but nothing. I laid the phone down next to me and waited again. Twenty minutes. Nothing again. At some point, my body gave up and I fell asleep.

But then, at about half past two, a vibration woke me. "I'm ok," the text read.

I responded right away: "why'd they do it?"

"Not u. I told them I wanted out."

"why?"

"u know why."

I paused. *Is he saying because of me? Or because of Gabby and Kwan? Or is it something else entirely?* I changed the subject.

"can we meet and talk?"

"Too risky."

"what do u mean?"

And then the phone vibrated. He was calling.

"Hi," I said shyly.

"Hi," he responded in a soft, tired voice that made my stomach flutter. "I thought it'd be a little difficult to explain all this through texting."

"Are you really okay?"

"That was nothing, Dresden. You should see the beating you get when you join the club."

"Sounds like a fun club," I said.

"I didn't admit to helping you with math, but they know,"

Sam said. "They saw your text to me after you got an A right before break. I told them you just got lucky, but I doubt they believed me. I think you'll be much safer if I ignore you."

"Is that why you haven't talked to me since you tutored me?"

"Yeah, exactly."

He'd been protecting me. Admittedly, I'd thought about what it would be like to kiss Sam Barrett, but now it was all I could think about. I tried to compose myself. "I guess I should say thank you, then," I said.

"No, you shouldn't. They still want you out of Hazelton, but I refuse to give them any reason to step up their game."

"Thanks."

"Did you get back your failing grade yet in Trig?"

"Oh, yeah."

"Sorry, that one slipped by me," he said.

"Barrett, that's not your fault. Besides, I handled that on my own."

He sounded surprised. "How?"

"Maybe I should just keep that to myself, in case someone's tapping your phone."

He laughed. "Okay. I guess I should go. These dorm walls are pretty thin."

"I'd say 'talk to you later,' but I guess that wouldn't make much sense," I said.

"I'll contact you, though, if I hear anything . . . if I can."

"You think they'll give up by tryouts?"

"I doubt it," he said. "But from what I hear, I'm not the only unhappy guy in the group."

"Well, at least someone else has a conscience."

"Yeah. Well, good luck, Dresden, with everything."

Yeah, good luck being alone for the rest of the year with no one to talk to. I wouldn't care about talking to anyone else if I could just talk to Sam. I wanted to say that, but all that came out was, "Sam?"

"Yeah?"

"Nothing. Thanks for calling."

After that call, I made a decision. I didn't need anybody's help. I'd get through this year on my own. I'd keep on doing what I'd been doing since the fall—sleep, study, workout, repeat.

But soon, the long cold days of a gray January turned into a February that looked and felt about the same. I became bitter and cold just like the weather. The lonelier I got, the angrier I got. I couldn't wait for the season to start so I could blow off some steam on the ball field.

Somehow, I badly needed that outlet.

Chapter 19

The second week in February, the halls were buzzing with talk of the upcoming Valentine's Day dance.

Mrs. Richards, as she had in October, insisted I go. She'd picked up on the fact that I spent all my time in my room studying or at the gym working out. "Come on, Taylor dear, you survived the Halloween dance, didn't you?"

Yeah, barely.

It was a week before baseball tryouts. I'd avoided two more attempts by the Statesmen to change my Trig grade, and I was carrying a solid B. Mr. Moesch had kept my secret, and he made sure he personally took my tests from my hand to avoid another "mix-up." Though I hadn't heard a word from Sam Barrett since January, I had managed not to go insane.

Just two days before, the Statesmen had upped their game. Dr. Colton called me into his office to tell me that there had been a student complaint about my behavior during practice. He said that a student, whose name was confidential, had told him I was being wild on the mound, intentionally injuring others. I assumed Grossman was the complainer, but he couldn't prove anything, and besides, it was just one wild pitch. And the whole thing had happened over a month ago. It was obvious the Statesmen were trying everything they could to get rid of me before tryouts.

I denied everything, and Dr. Colton said this would serve as a warning, since none of the coaches could confirm the story. If he had any further complaints, he would have to take further action. Dr. Rich spoke to me about it as well. I figured I would have to find another way to fight back, besides beaning the bastards one at a time. The whole thing was making me angrier by the day, and I now started to feel it was an accomplishment that I had survived against the Statesmen this long.

My survival called for a celebration, but what kind of fool would go back to the scene of the crime? In the recesses of my mind, I had to admit I wanted to go to the Valentine's Day dance, if only to satisfy my curiosity about what the Statesmen would do—and also to get a chance to stare at Sam.

I couldn't wait for baseball season to start. It was so much easier than all this complicated social life stuff.

And that's when it hit me. The Statesmen got me at a dance last time. Maybe this was the perfect opportunity for revenge. That was the best reason of all to show up.

But what can I do? I tried to think of something that, if they got caught doing it, they could get thrown out of school. They were always trying to get me thrown out—they deserved a taste of their own medicine. Unfortunately, I did not know where to get drugs of any sort, as the Statesmen obviously did, so drugging someone was out of the question.

Besides, I didn't think I had the guts to pull that off. Still, if one of the Statesmen got caught with alcohol, or even cigarettes, for that matter, I'm sure they would be severely disciplined, and maybe even expelled. *But where can I get something like that?*

And then I remembered the last place I had seen a pack of cigarettes—in Gabby's boyfriend's hand. Jordan smoked. I picked my cell phone up and dialed Gabby's number. Gabby deserved a hand in my payback.

"Gab, Jordan smokes, right?"

"Yeah. I'm trying to get him to quit, but he's totally bullheaded. Why?"

An hour and a half later, Jordan's car was pulling up next to the Hazelton entrance gates and I had my contraband. This was going to be fun.

I decided that whichever Statesmen jerk I could get closest to would end up with the pack in his jacket pocket. I was hoping for Tuttle or Ben, but any Statesman would do. Then I would just drop Dr. Rich a subtle hint that I smelled smoke, and things would move quickly from there. I would take them out one at a time, just like they did with Gabby and Kwan.

Out the door I went around eight o'clock, the cigarettes hidden deep inside the little purse I decided to carry. I wore the strap across my chest to free up my hands, and to keep the pack close to me. Dr. and Mrs. Richards were chaperoning, so I helped them carry over some Valentine's cupcakes. Helping them set up a table would give me something to do, and it'd be a good cover, too, I figured.

I'd decided not to get all dolled up this time. I just wore a pair of skinny jeans with my favorite tall black leather boots and a long, black v-neck sweater that Justin had given me the previous Christmas. I'd retrieved from my top drawer my necklace with the bear sign on it. I figured I needed it for good luck.

The place was more packed than it had been for Halloween. There were a lot more girls milling around, hunting for sons of rich men to sink their claws into. I followed Dr. and Mrs. Richards over to a table with the cupcakes.

"Taylor?" Mrs. Richards said. I turned around to see a very

petite girl with shoulder-length red hair smiling at me. She was carrying a tray of heart-shaped cookies. "I want you to meet my niece, Marielle."

"Hi," I said, taking the tray from her.

"Hi," she said cheerily.

"Marielle goes to school a few towns over in Maplewood."

"Nice to meet you," I said, and I sincerely meant it. It was nice to have the possibility of someone to talk to tonight.

"Can I help you guys set up?" Marielle asked.

"Yeah, sure," I said. "We need to get the napkins and tablecloth out of the bag over there." I pointed behind the table.

"Anything so I don't look desperate and lonely," she said.

"I hear you," I said, smiling. I scanned the room for my targets. I spotted Tuttle and Grossman, but no Ben. I figured I'd wait until the place crowded up more before making any moves.

For the first hour, I hung out with Marielle and Dr. and Mrs. Richards, sitting on folding chairs by their table while eating cupcakes and candy. It wasn't the ideal evening, but it was shaping up as better than the last dance. Marielle and I talked about school—she was a junior—and at length about boys. When that topic came up, I scanned the room for Sam.

"Isn't it hard to be around all these good-looking guys all day?" she asked.

Just one. "Not really," I said. "Most of them despise me."

"Really? Why?"

"'Cause they're snotty spoiled brats, I guess. But don't worry. They'll get theirs."

"What do you mean?" She seemed shocked by my comment.

I didn't know Marielle well enough to inform her of my

plan for the evening. "Nothing," I said. "What goes around comes around."

"Someone's got anger issues," Marielle said as she scarfed down another cookie.

I took a swig of my soda. "Yeah, well, if you had any idea what they've done to torture me, you'd understand why I'm angry."

"So why let their immaturity ruin you?"

"Huh?"

"Well, I find that if I'm bothered when people are jerks to me, that means they win and I just feel like crap. Don't let other people bring you down. It should give you more of a reason to rise up. Revenge may feel good for the moment, but regret lasts forever." Her comments reminded me of that book, *The Count of Monte Cristo*, that I'd read in the fall. The main character succeeded in the end, but he still seemed sad and jaded.

"And how is it that you're so wise beyond your years?" I said, now questioning my cigarette-pack plan.

"Having two kidney transplants before you're sixteen will do that, you know. It'll give you a lot of theories about life."

Here I was, complaining about my situation, and this girl obviously had serious health problems. "Wow, I must sound like a whiny bitch, huh?"

"No, you don't. You've been here by yourself all this time. You're using your anger to help you survive. But there are other ways to make it through tough times."

Marielle made sense. Why should I let this whole situation bring me down? I'd spent my first few teenage years angry. I shouldn't do that again. "You have a point. I'll be right back," I said, heading toward the hall, where I wrapped the pack of cigarettes in a wad of tissue paper and buried it in the garbage can. It was a stupid idea anyway, and I could be caught with the cigarettes as easily as a Statesman.

Besides, I wasn't the revenge type after all. I was stronger than that.

As I returned to the cupcake table, the lights dimmed for a slow dance, and couples paired off in front of us. A guy came over and asked Marielle to dance. She beamed. "Do you mind, Taylor?"

"No way. Knock yourself out."

She disappeared into the darkness. I folded my arms and leaned back in my chair. I was happy someone had asked her to dance. She deserved it.

"Would *you* like to dance?" a voice asked from behind me.

I turned around, and there, leaning against the wall, was Sam.

"Yeah, right," I said, laughing at him and turning back around so no one would see us talking.

"I'm serious." He sat down next to me.

"Aren't you still protecting me with the silent treatment?"

"Yeah, well," he said, grabbing my hand and pulling me out of my seat, "I'm taking the night off."

"Sam," I said, letting him drag me toward the dance floor, "are you crazy? People will see."

"I really don't care anymore."

What in the world is happening? I put my arms around him and we started to move to the music. *Am I hallucinating? Is Sam Barrett actually dancing with me?* "You don't care anymore, huh?"

"Nope."

"Why not?"

"I just figured that, one, I've told them, over and over, that

I refuse to rejoin the club—they can only beat me up so many times before they get tired of it. And, two, it's Valentine's Day, and I wanted to dance with you."

"You wanted to dance with *me?*" I said.

"Yes, I did."

"Why?"

He whispered in my ear, "Because I like you, Dresden. Now stop talking and dance."

And that's just what we did. I figured I would enjoy the attention while it lasted. Being that close to his face, I was afraid to really look at him, so I focused on his shoulder instead. He lightly held one of my hands and placed his other hand on the middle of my back. He was the perfect gentleman.

I found exhaling difficult, and I didn't know if I could hold my breath for a whole song, but apparently I could. As we swayed to the music, I glanced at the crowd of people dancing nearby, hoping I could see their reactions. A couple of younger guys, probably sophomores, smiled in our direction.

When the song ended, Sam stepped back and simply said, "Thanks for the dance." He winked at me and tipped an imaginary hat. "Good luck next week." And then, in usual Sam form, he was gone.

I watched him cross the gymnasium, where a guy slapped hands with him, as if he were impressed that Sam had had the courage to dance with me. I recognized the guy, Clifton, as the same one who'd asked me if Sam was okay after the fight. *Maybe it's true. Maybe they're not all Statesmen. Maybe there are other guys who hate the Statesmen as much as I do.*

That night, I dug out Sam's t-shirt from my bottom dresser drawer and put it on. I was glad I hadn't thrown it away. I think I smiled.

I was supposed to meet my mother the next day for breakfast, but I wasn't at all nervous. Something lulled me into a peaceful sleep.

Chapter 20

The next morning's plan, as arranged by Dad, was for me to have breakfast with my mom at Dock's Pancake House. It was a log cabin-like restaurant right in downtown Hazelton.

Mrs. Richards drove me, and all I told her was that I was getting together with my mother. I left out the part that I hadn't seen her since I was five. I didn't want Mrs. Richards to ask me if I wanted to talk about it later or pat my hand and offer to make some tea for me back at the house.

I closed the door to Mrs. Richards's minivan. Then I stood outside the pancake house and looked around, though I honestly wasn't sure if I'd recognize her. *Does she look the same as in those old pictures?*

After a few minutes, I was getting cold and figured maybe she'd already gone inside. I took a deep breath and opened the big wooden door to the restaurant.

The place was packed. All around me, forks clanked against ceramic plates, and the cash register chugged out receipts. Dad said she would find me. He'd sent her some recent pictures, and she'd told him she'd been following my high school baseball career.

"Taylor," said a woman a few feet to my left. Then I felt a light touch on the arm of my jacket.

I turned around and was amazed. Her face was exactly as I had recalled. I guess I remembered more than I thought I would.

She was tall and very thin. Her dark brown hair was pulled back in a loose ponytail. She had on just enough makeup to make her face seem awake and fresh without being too painted up. In fact, her style seemed a lot like mine. She looked sweet and kind, not like a woman who left her husband for another man, or to live the party life.

"Hi," I said, leaving off the "Mom" part just because I wasn't sure if either of us was ready for that.

"I got us a booth over here by the window," she said. "Do you drink coffee?"

And with that, I knew this was going to be a good meeting. I smiled and said, "Caffeine is my middle name."

"I second that," she said as the waitress approached. "Two regular coffees, please."

She asked me about school and baseball. Oddly enough, there were no uncomfortable silences. This intrigued me, because I usually had trouble talking to other girls. Maybe it was because she was a grownup, or because she was, after all, my mother.

We ate pancakes with strawberries and drank a few more cups of coffee. I held the warm cup in my cold fingers and answered all of her questions. I wanted to ask questions of my own, but I realized I didn't have to do everything at one breakfast, unless for some reason she got depressed again.

So I settled for the one question I had always wanted to ask her. The dishes had been cleared and I knew I was up against the clock. "Can I just ask you one thing?"

"Of course," she said.

"I apologize for just coming right out with this, but it's been like a dozen years since I've seen you, so I—"

"Just ask, Taylor. It's fine."

"Why'd you leave?"

She put her head in her hands and stared at me for a few moments before letting out a huge sigh. "I've been through a lot of years of therapy because of what I did to you kids. I've never forgiven myself for that. I was a sick person, Taylor," she said. "I didn't know what was wrong with me then. It was many years later, after many breakdowns, that I was diagnosed with bipolar disorder, which basically means that most of the time I feel sad, but I have the occasional overly happy day. I couldn't control what I was doing back then. The whole thing is like a long blur. But mental illness or not, what I did to you was wrong and I am truly sorry."

"But you're better now?"

"Today is a good day. I can only take one day at a time, but this time I'm really fighting for myself."

I didn't understand what her disorder was. It sounded kind of made up, but I didn't want to be rude. *Bipolar? Sounds like some sort of bear.* She seemed sincere enough about it all. I believed her when she said she hadn't forgiven herself. I wasn't going to say that it was okay and that I forgave her, so I just said, "Thanks for answering my question."

"Of course, and thanks so much for agreeing to meet with me today. Do you think we could do it again sometime?"

I didn't know what this woman, who I hadn't seen for most of my life, would now become for me. I didn't think we'd become best friends, go shopping together, and talk on the phone every day, but a little relationship seemed better than none at all. At least I thought it did. "Yeah, sure."

"How about we do it again next month? I'd be happy to pick you up at school, or we could just meet somewhere again."

"Uh, maybe, yeah, I'll think about it. How about you call me?"

I gave my mother my cell number. How weird was that? My mother didn't know my phone number! She paid the bill and walked me to the door.

We said our goodbyes inside the restaurant. I gave her a quick no-pressure hug. I didn't have a ride home, so I figured I'd just walk. I could use the exercise. Although it was really cold, I didn't want to walk out with her and have her feel pressured into giving me a ride. All the way back, my mind was focused on the cold, which was good because it kept me from overanalyzing the meeting.

Tryouts were scheduled for Wednesday, after school. I was ready. In my corner now were two new people—my mom and Sam.

I hoped so, anyway.

Chapter 21

It was the day of tryouts. I couldn't focus in school at all. I sat in the café at lunch, trying to force down a turkey sandwich. I had to eat to get my energy level up, but my stomach was churning. Madison and Sabatini had said that tryouts were really just a formality for me, but at Hazelton, everyone had to try out, whether they were on scholarship or not. I knew I was good, and I had seen a few other junior pitchers working out with Madison who didn't seem to pose much of a threat, but I still didn't want to mess up. Everybody has an occasional bad day on the mound. I just hoped today wasn't my turn.

I saw Tuttle storm into the café. He seemed perturbed about something. He huddled with his Statesmen group for a few minutes. I flipped through the pages of the new book I had for English, *Of Mice and Men,* by John Steinbeck. I was happy to see it was only one hundred pages long.

I wondered how men could be like mice, but my thoughts were interrupted when I saw Tuttle coming toward me. *What the hell does he want? If he were a mouse, I would snap his head off in a trap.* I should have known he was going to try to rattle me on tryout day. As he approached, I braced myself.

"Hey, Dresden," he said, acting casual, "I saw you on the list for tryouts today."

"So?" I asked, trying to remain mellow and calm.

"You know that anyone carrying below a C-minus in any course can't try out, right?"

"Yeah, so?" I said, sounding pissed.

"Well, aren't you failing Trig?"

"Uh, excuse me, but are we friends or something now? Why so concerned with my grades all of a sudden? I don't remember discussing them with you in the past."

He knew that I knew he had messed with my quizzes. But what he didn't know was that I had fixed everything with Mr. Moesch. I could see him putting it all together in his head. His expression changed.

We stood there in silence for a moment. Then, from out of nowhere, two underclassmen stepped casually between Tuttle and me, acting as if they hadn't realized they were walking into a confrontation.

"Oh, excuse me, Dresden," said the shorter of the two boys before continuing on his path across the café. I didn't know him, but there was something in this guy's gesture that struck me. He said "excuse me" to *me*, not to Tuttle, king of the Statesmen. He said it to me! I felt empowered.

They're not all Statesmen.

I gathered my things and stood up. Getting close to Tuttle's face, I said, "Two can play at your game, Tuttle." Then I walked a few paces from him before turning and adding, "See you on the field today. Good luck." *You're going to need it.*

Later that afternoon, I set off to change into my tryout outfit. It was still bitterly cold out, and though we practiced in the bubble, tryouts would be on one of the outdoor practice fields. I went into the ladies' room and put on the gray uniform pants I'd saved from my old school. I slipped on a tight, white thermal shirt, and then a red jersey t-shirt I'd worn last year for tryouts. I figured it would give me some good luck.

From my bag, I pulled out my good luck bear-charm necklace and fastened it around my neck. Then I slipped my feet into my black and white cleats. I pulled my hair back into a ponytail and then through the back of the old red Phillies hat my grandpa had given me after I'd pitched my first no-hitter. I didn't usually braid my ponytail, but I decided to do it today. Getting struck out by a girl was bad enough, but a braid would just twist the knife in the wound a little more.

You can do this, Taylor. I leaned on the sink and stared at myself in the mirror. *Relax, this is what you want—a challenge.* Then came a knock on the door.

"Be done in a minute!" I yelled.

Again, the knock. "Taylor, it's me, Sam. Open up," he whispered.

I cracked open the door. "What are you doing here?"

"Come with me a minute," he said, opening the door wider.

"Uh, okay," I said, following him down the hall.

He opened the door to the equipment closet. "In here," he said, motioning, looking down the hall to make sure no one was watching us. I stepped inside and he quickly closed the door.

I sat on a stack of floor mats. "What's up?" I asked, confused. I hadn't talked to him since the Valentine's Day dance.

"Just want to tell you to be careful. The guys are pissed about the Trig thing."

"I'll be fine, Barrett. Don't worry."

He paced around before sitting down next to me. "I'm not in the loop anymore, so I don't know what they may do." He was obviously upset.

I patted his hand. "Don't worry, I'm a big girl. I can take care of myself."

"Well, if you can't, I've got your back."

"Thanks. I'm sure I'll be fine."

We sat quietly for a few moments. I kicked my feet against the mat a couple of times. He turned and looked me up and down and smiled.

"What?" I asked.

"Nothing. You look cute in your whole uniform thing."

I blushed and looked down at my feet. "Shut up."

"No, you do," he said.

"Thanks, I guess," I muttered, still staring at my feet.

"I'm serious. You really do," he said. And then, he slowly put his finger under my chin and lifted it up. *Oh my god, he's going to kiss me.*

"I didn't plan on doing this when I brought you in here, but I can't help myself." He moved his face toward mine and I met him halfway. His lips were so soft. My body temperature went up a few degrees as he kissed me.

"Are you trying to ruin me for tryouts?" I asked after our kiss ended.

"Sorry. Yeah, you're right. We should save our adrenaline for the field, huh?"

I stood up and agreed, "Yeah, we should."

"Maybe we could meet up after?" he said.

"Dude, you're killing me," I said. "Could you just act like you hate me for the next few hours? I need to be a rock and you're turning me into Play-Doh, acting like this."

"Sorry."

"Did the Statesmen tell you to kiss me to mess with my head?" I said. He stood next to me and shook his head before trying to kiss me again. "Not fair," I said, stepping back.

"Oh, right, act like I hate you. I got it." He walked quickly toward the door and opened it. Then he yelled back to me, trying not to laugh, "And another thing, Dresden. You suck!"

I couldn't help myself. I laughed.

Tryouts were anything but funny. I'd never been through such an exhausting round. There were a total of eight people trying out for pitcher. Three would make varsity, three would make JV, and two would be cut. The coaches started everyone with a few laps around the field. They paired up all the pitchers with catchers, and a group of coaches walked around observing each pair.

Then came the batters. The coaches made all the pitchers face a whole lineup of hitters. The first three guys gave up a few hits. Tuttle was fourth to pitch, and he hadn't given up a hit yet. For some reason, I was set to pitch last. I overheard one of the pitchers complaining that the batters would be tired by then and I'd have it easy.

I called him out on his crap. "What number are you?"

"Fifth," he said, flashing his number at me.

I grabbed it and tossed him mine. "Here, now you're eighth, smart ass."

"Uh, I didn't mean—"

I walked away before he had a chance to argue. I refused to let anyone think I was getting on this team just because I was a girl.

Then, all of a sudden, I was up. I passed Tuttle, who in the end surrendered only one hit, as he walked down into the dugout. He decided to shift sideways, forcing me to dodge right. Class act, that Tuttle.

I took my spot on the mound. The first guy went down in three pitches. The second batter took a ball, then swung like a madman and missed my next three fastballs. The third guy made contact with my second pitch and fouled it back, but that was the only contact he made.

The fourth batter was Sam. When I saw him approach the batter's box, I forced back all inclinations to smile. I also tried to forget what had just happened in the equipment room.

He stood on the left side of the plate. *What are you doing on that side? You know righty is your stronger side. Trying to make it easy for me, are you?* I stepped off the mound and signaled Coach Madison. He jogged out quickly. "What's up?"

"May I request that he bat righty?"

Madison knew why. "Gotta love a girl who loves a challenge," he said. He whistled at Barrett and pointed. "Other side, Barrett."

Sam shook his head and smiled as he switched sides. I began my delivery. Ball one. *Shoot.* Curve ball, strike one. He just watched that one.

Next one, fly ball, deep left field.

Caught.

The next four batters went down easily. I was the first pitcher not to give up a hit. I went back to the dugout.

Madison nodded and tapped me on the shoulder with his clipboard. "Impressive," he whispered.

I stuck around and watched the rest of the pitchers. Pitcher number eight got roped. I guess the batters weren't tired after all.

Once everyone had finished, Barrett caught up to me as I

walked off the field.

"I *will* strike you out one day, Barrett," I said.

"Too bad we're playing on the same team."

"There's always batting practice," I said. I kept a good distance from him. I didn't know who could be watching.

"You're on, Dresden," he said, closing the gap between us.

"So, should we talk about what happened earlier in the equipment room?"

"Yeah, I'd love to," he said, nudging my arm.

I was surprised he was confident enough to touch me in public. "Well, what does it all mean?" I asked.

"Hmm, what does it mean?" he said. He pretended to mull it over. "It means whatever you want it to mean, I guess. I don't want to put any pressure on you. I just know if I do that again with anyone anytime soon, I hope that someone is you."

"What about all the Statesmen?"

He shrugged. "Who?"

I wasn't sure if this meant Sam Barrett and I were a thing, or going out, or what, but I had to focus on baseball right now and prepare for the scouts. I decided to relax about Sam and let whatever was going to happen just happen.

Chapter 22

That Friday, the list of people who made the varsity team was posted outside the gym. I heard it was put up after lunch, but I didn't want to look while surrounded by a big crowd of guys. I figured I would wait until later. I did really well in tryouts, but I still felt nervous that the Statesmen might have messed it all up somehow. *What if they're powerful enough to fix it so I don't make the team? I'd have spent all this time here suffering alone for nothing. No scout will ever see me. I'll never get into a decent college.*

I felt nauseated, but I kept my distance from the gym. I wanted to see that list when no one was watching.

I had asked Sam to keep our relationship quiet in school, because I didn't want to draw any more attention to myself. But he still sent me a text once or twice a day that kept me smiling. Shortly after the list was up, a text came in.

"See the list?"

"Nope."

"Go look."

"Later."

"Want me to tell u?"

"NO!"

"Ok, text me."

During study period, I couldn't take it anymore. I asked

to use the bathroom and hustled toward the gym. I stared up at the long list of varsity names on the door: "Atkins, Barrett, Brown, Dunnell, Dresden . . ."

"Yes!" I said, slapping my hands together. *Yes, yes, yes.* The last few months of solitude, torture, and studying had all been worth it.

I ducked into the nearest ladies' bathroom, took out my cell, and dialed my dad at work. "Dad, I did it. I made the team!" I exclaimed, excited.

"Of course you did," he replied happily.

Daily practice began the following week, and it was a killer. I was so tired afterward that sometimes I fell asleep in my room before 9 p.m. My muscles had never hurt so bad and been so happy at the same time. Things were finally going my way.

Then came our first practice game.

The junior varsity and the varsity were to scrimmage against one another. Although it was obvious that the varsity team would win, it was a good way to allow the teams to play together, and for the players to get to know each other as a team. We were set to play the full seven innings. I wasn't scheduled to start, but the coaches said they were going to field everybody.

I really wanted to start. I'd been a reliever all summer, but I wasn't fond of that role. Starters were, in my opinion, the *real* pitchers. Closers and relievers just had a lot of heat. I liked the feeling I used to get sticking it out for the whole game. It took stamina to go the distance, to wear the other team down, one batter at a time. I wanted to be a starter. When the time was right, I was going to mention that to Madison.

Most of the varsity team—my team—was made up of juniors and seniors. I'd seen most of the guys in class and, to my knowledge, the only Statesmen on the varsity team were Sam, who had recently resigned from the group, Grossman, Roberts, and my "friend," William Tuttle. At least I knew I wouldn't have to be on the field at the same time as him. Of course, I might have to relieve him, or vice versa, and that would be, well, interesting.

I figured I'd made it this far, and I knew, although he was one of the four Statesmen who beat up Sam, that alone, Tuttle was intimidated by Sam. He had obviously spent the last four years looking up to him, and I sensed he still knew that Sam was somehow superior. Sam had moved on with his life, grown too mature for the whole evil clique, and Tuttle was jealous. He was looking to prove himself. As I watched him enter the gym, I thought that maybe I was in trouble.

Before the game, we all met inside the gym with the coaches. They were treating the scrimmage like a real game, going over game plans, giving us the lineup that would probably remain for the season. Barrett was the leadoff man. Tuttle was starting pitcher.

"All right, get in uniform and meet us outside on the field. It's cold out there, so dress warmly, especially you pitchers," Coach Houghton said.

There was still no locker room for me to use, so I went out into the hall and down past the equipment room to the ladies' room. I changed into my Hazelton practice uniform. (Yes, this school actually had practice uniforms for scrimmages. Must be nice to be filthy rich.) The shirt was blue, and across the front was the word "Hazelton." On the side of the sleeves was a big "V" for Varsity.

I was all set and ready to go. I unlocked the bathroom door and tried to pull it open. It wouldn't budge. I tried to lock and unlock it again, but it still wouldn't open. I yanked and threw my shoulder into it, trying to release it, but then the handle fell off and onto the floor. It had cracked in half and the handle on the outside of the door was still on, so I couldn't even see into the hallway. *Drat!*

I was locked in here, and no one was close enough to hear me. I banged for a while. "Hello!" I yelled. "Anybody? Hello?" Just silence.

And then it hit me. *The Statesmen. They must have messed with the door handle and locked me in.* I panicked and looked around the room. There was no window—no other way out.

I heard a clicking noise on the outside of the door.

"Hello? Somebody there?"

The door opened just a bit. I reached for the door, wedging my hand into the crack.

Then the door pulled shut from the other side, slamming my hand between the door and the wall. "Ow!" I screamed, unable to release my hand, feeling my fingers being crushed by the door. "Let go, let go!" I yelled.

I heard a loud thud, and suddenly my hand was free again. I opened the door to see Sam knocking William Tuttle to the floor.

"What the hell is wrong with you?!" Sam yelled at him. "You could've broken her hand!" He grabbed the front of Tuttle's shirt. "Enough is enough!" Sam brought his hand back, ready to punch him again.

"Stop!" a voice yelled from down the hall. "Break it up, gentlemen!" Coach Madison and Dr. Colton ran toward us and separated the two boys.

Sam turned to Dr. Colton. "I apologize, sir, but if you knew what he was trying to—"

"We know what he was trying to do," Coach Madison said. "We saw the whole thing." I stood dumbfounded in the doorway. "Dresden, are you all right?"

I nodded. "Yeah, I'm okay."

"Have a nurse take a look at that, just in case," said Dr. Colton. "Mr. Barrett, please walk her down to the nurse's office while I deal with Mr. Tuttle."

"Sir, this is all a big misunderstanding," said Tuttle.

"Quiet, Mr. Tuttle. If you know what's good for you, you will close your mouth this instant! We do not tolerate violence at Hazelton. We do not need students like you at this institution."

Sam was pulling me down the hall, away from the action. "You sure you're okay?"

"Yeah, I'm fine." My hand was certainly bruised, and it did hurt, but I didn't think anything was broken.

I'd probably be okay to pitch, the nurse told me. I just needed to take it easy.

As for Tuttle playing in the game, well, that never happened. Madison had a junior named West start and Tuttle was sent back to his dormitory room.

Chapter 23

I was unsure if I could focus enough to take the mound that day, but I rejoined the team in the dugout. It was obvious the coaches and players knew what had happened. Word traveled fast at Hazelton. Although most of the players sat quietly, a few of the guys tipped their hats to me and nodded when I walked by. They were obviously not fans of Tuttle.

One of the catchers, Dunnell, walked up to me and tossed a ball into my glove. "Good luck today, Dresden," he said. Their gestures and kind words actually seemed sincere, but maybe I was just hallucinating because of the day's drama.

Coach Madison pulled me aside and whispered, "Don't let it rattle you, Dresden. You have to separate all the stupid crap that's going to happen to you in your life and keep yourself focused on what you want. You hear me?"

I nodded. "I got it, Coach. You're right. I'll be fine." *I think.*

And as it turned out, I was. I went in after the fourth inning and finished the game. It was just a scrimmage, but it definitely helped that Madison made me get right back on the horse. He didn't give me time to get scared—scared that someone else might try to crush the dream I'd worked so hard for.

As Sam walked me off the field, one of the guys hanging by the bleachers yelled, "You got game, Dresden! Woo!" We both cracked a smile at that one.

After the game, I was told I had to go and speak to the headmaster. As I walked back to the main building, I felt myself start to shake a bit. It could have been the fear that someone had actually tried to physically hurt me. Or maybe it was just the cold.

Dr. Colton didn't waste any time getting to the point. "Miss Dresden, let me first apologize for Mr. Tuttle's attack," he said. "I assure you, you will not see his face here at Hazelton again."

"It's good to hear I have one less enemy."

"Is there some reason he would have attacked you in this way?"

'Cause he's a jackass. "He just didn't want me on his team, I suppose."

"Well, I put a call in to your father to let him know about the incident, but he was not available," said Dr. Colton. "When he calls back, I will explain how truly sorry we are here at Hazelton for your mistreatment."

"You called my dad?" I asked nervously.

"Yes."

"Why did you have to do that?"

"I have an obligation to keep him informed of the situation."

"Could you do me a favor and let me tell him what happened?" I asked.

"Don't worry, Miss Dresden. You're not in trouble."

"I know that. I just think my dad will handle it better if it comes from me— that's all." *I want him to think I'm fine. I want him to think I belong here. I want him to be proud of me.*

"I feel as if there's something you're not telling me, Miss Dresden," said Dr. Colton.

I fidgeted in my seat. My head began to pound and my pulse quickened as I prepared to spill my guts. Enough was enough. I nervously cracked my knuckles, took a deep breath, and let it out. "Sir, do you know there's a clique at this school that William Tuttle was part of?" I said.

"A clique?" he asked.

I nodded. "They're a group of upperclassmen who seem to want things their way, and one of the things they wanted was to get rid of me."

I was surprised when he said, "Unfortunately, in the weeks since the whole incident with Miss Kwan, I've been hearing things that mirror what you're telling me. And after what happened today with you and Mr. Tuttle, I am going to make a serious effort at putting a stop to any malfeasance."

Malfeasance? I had to ask. "You mean you're going to get the bad guys?" I asked.

"Yes, Miss Dresden," he said, laughing slightly. "Precisely. And if you feel more comfortable explaining things to your father first, that's fine. Just have him call me tomorrow to confirm that the two of you spoke."

I had to say something about Gabby. "Dr. Colton?"

"Yes, Miss Dresden?"

"I think the whole thing with Gabby Foster may have had something to do with Tuttle, too, sir."

"I will give Miss Foster a call this evening. Maybe I owe her an apology."

"Thank you, sir. I really appreciate that." I rose to leave. "And seriously, thank you for letting me come to Hazelton. Really, I have learned so much about everything—not just baseball, but a million other things."

And I meant it. Although I'd been brought here as a publicity stunt, I didn't care. Without this place, I never would have learned Trig, or finished an entire novel, or been coached by a professional ballplayer, or learned how to survive on my own, or met Sam. No matter what the circumstances were for bringing me here, I was glad I'd come. I was grateful, too.

Sam was waiting for me outside the headmaster's office. He was still in his uniform, sitting on a stone wall, his legs half-blocking the plaque that read, "The Hazelton School: Where Boys Become Men." *Well, at least one of them did,* I thought, looking at Sam. "I can't thank you enough for what you did for me today," I said.

"You'd have done the same thing for me. And honestly, so would a lot of the guys around here."

"I don't know. Maybe."

"It's true. You saw some of the guys in the dugout today. They were happy to see a Statesman get in trouble. And since I quit the Statesmen, I've noticed something," Sam said. "Many of those quiet, nerdy guys who hide in the library, or even some of the new guys on the team I may not have known so well—they're all really good people. It's like they all hated Tuttle and the Statesmen, and I guess me as well, at one time. And I don't blame them for hating them . . . for hating us. Who wants to live in fear or feel like they're not as good? School shouldn't be about that. Maybe things are finally going to change around here."

"And all because of you," I said.

"Not because of me. Because of you," he said. "If you'd never come here, I'd probably still be the same guy, a Statesman, trying to dictate how everything should be. Too bad I'm a senior. I'm finally starting to like this place."

"Well, there's always college." I nudged his shoulders. "And there are girls there, too."

He smiled and shook his head. "Speaking of which, I know things have been a crazy rollercoaster ride with us, but maybe we can come to some sort of understanding. I would never want to mess with your ability to pitch."

"What are you talking about?" I said.

"Except when we're on the field together, we can be like boyfriend and girlfriend."

This is too good to be true. "How about practice?" I said.

He rubbed his chin, thinking. "Practice would be hands-off, I think."

"How about in the gym?"

"The gym is hands-off, too, but the bus rides after practices and after games are open to discussion." He stood and took my hand. "And then, after each game, we'll walk across campus together, holding hands, and you're going to tell me how great I was on the field."

"Is that right?"

"Yup."

I wasn't going to argue. He'd proven himself time and again with me. I was sold.

When I got back to the house that night, I was surprised when Mrs. Richards told me my dad was waiting for me in Dr. Rich's office. I rushed in to see him.

"Dad, what are you doing here?" I said, reaching for a hug.

"I got a voice mail from Dr. Colton and I didn't like the tone of his voice," Dad said. "I was on the road anyway, driving back from a meeting in Ewing, so I figured I'd drive over."

"Dad, Ewing is, like, thirty miles from here."

"Yeah, well, I was worried about my daughter, so shoot me. What exactly happened? Dr. Colton said there was an incident."

I had spilled my guts to Dr. Colton, and now it was time to do the same with my dad. He deserved to know the truth, about everything—the Statesmen, Sam, Gabby, everything.

I closed the office door.

After I told my dad the long, complicated tale of my past six months at Hazelton, I assured him that Dr. Colton was going to put an end to the Statesmen and that I was safe now.

"So, after all of this, you still want to stay here?" he asked.

"Yeah," I said, nodding. "I do."

"I guess my little girl has grown up a lot this year, huh?"

"In more ways than one."

Dad gave me a big bear hug and said, "So, just one more question."

"What's that?" I said.

"When's your first game?"

As I pulled the comforter over me that night, I felt a wave of relief. For the first time, I felt safe and welcome at Hazelton. I looked up at the hats hanging on the wall. *That old red one is all mine now. I am so wearing that tomorrow.*

After the Tuttle incident, it took a while for the air to clear. In fact, the stench of the Statesmen hung in the halls for a few weeks. Surprisingly, Sam said the remaining Statesmen were trying to regroup and keep their clique alive, but with little success. Many guys feared expulsion after what had happened to Tuttle. Things were dying down. Sam's brother, Ben, even apologized to me one day in the café. I accepted it, but I'm sure Sam had threatened to kick his butt if he didn't.

Enough of this drama, enough worrying about boys, enough failing classes, enough fighting Statesmen. It's time to do what I do best. Pitch.

After months of confusion, I finally felt I had my focus back.

Chapter 24

The first game of the season, all of them were there—the scouts, that is. Some were from the west coast, some from the south and southeast. Texas, Miami, Arizona, and even major league farm teams were present. I had never seen anything like it. Also in the stands were the Richards family, my dad and brother, and half the student body. And I even noticed a friendly face sitting on the field level and waving. It was Gabby, who must have received and accepted Dr. Colton's apology.

My mom had called earlier to wish me good luck, and I decided I'd meet her again for breakfast. We might even make it a monthly thing, I thought.

I was scheduled to start—Coach Madison was convinced I was ready for anything after walking onto the field and keeping my focus even after that jerk crushed my hand in a door. Coach had told me that day, "I know you're a girl and all, but you got balls." Clearly, that's one of my top ten favorite compliments ever from a coach.

We were facing St. Joe's, a prep school whose head coach, I heard, had phoned earlier to see if the rumor of a girl pitcher was actually true. "Not only is the rumor true, but we're starting her against your boys today," was Madison's response.

With Tuttle gone, there was a cheery mood in our dugout.

The guys talked to me not like I was a girl, but like I was a teammate. That made throwing the first pitch a whole lot easier, knowing that the team was behind me.

Sam was safely tucked in left field, and I knew he would always have my back. I laughed inside when I thought about how much I had once loathed him. He had thanked me for making him a better person, but I knew he'd only himself to thank. You can't change someone. They have to want to change themselves. Sam wanted to change.

Madison assured me that someone inevitably would get a hit off me today, because these guys were good. "Don't let it rattle you," he said. "You've been playing against much less talented teams for years, so a hit is bound to come."

He was right. I had to leave my safety zone if I wanted to go somewhere with my pitching. And, I hoped, that somewhere would be college.

I stood on the mound and readied myself for the first pitch. I blocked everyone out and just went to that place—that safe place—where I love baseball, where my dad is cheering for me, where my brother is telling jokes, and where everything is in perfect rhythm.

And then I delivered my first pitch for Hazelton. The crowd erupted as the batter swung and missed. I was on top of the world.

We won the game, four to one. I gave up two hits, walked two, and struck out eight in the five innings I pitched—not bad for my first time starting on a real team.

After the game, I shook a lot of hands, including that of a scout from the University of Miami who seemed extremely happy to meet me.

Miami—warm weather, the beach, and baseball year-round.

Pretty good deal, right?

But I decided to keep my options open. Who knew what else might change before the season was over?

I'm a bird with wings
And I can fly.
I stretch my wings out wide,
I'm so high up in the sky
When I fly, I feel free.
Free of sadness and anger
All I'm filled with is glee.

—*Marielle Bakri (1995-2008)*

Acknowledgements

Thank you to the fine people at Bancroft Press, especially Bruce Bortz for believing Taylor Dresden had another story to tell; Harrison Demchick and Julie Steinbacher for their fabulous suggestions and editing; and Tracy Copes for creating a beautiful front cover.

Thank you to those who have always supported my writing career: the Griffiths family, the Moesch family, the Kirby family, the Buono family, the Robertson family, the Lyons family, the Cloutier family, the Ciccotello family, the Gilsenan family, Jeanne Doremus, Ed and Pat Nicholanco, Leah Mustra, and Stephanie Konschak.

Thank you to all the staff and students at South Orange Middle School who make school a fun place to be, especially: Dan Savarese, Ellen Hark, Fran Cristalli, Ashley Griffin, Steven Cohen, Bernadine Smith, Kathy Hester, Liz Harris, Marty Weber, Kathleen Andersen, Bonnie DiBlasio, Gayle Martone, Debra Myers, Carla Dos Santos, Danielle Levine, Becky Donahue, and Gary Pankiewicz.

Thank you to Jamie and Benjamin for their love and support.

To Marielle Bakri, to whom this book is dedicated, thank you for sharing your writing and yourself with me and inspiring so many people.

Many thanks to the Bakri family for sharing Marielle's words with me.

About the Author

Sara Griffiths is a young adult author and teacher. Her first novel, *Thrown A Curve,* was published in May 2007. Sara has been teaching language arts to seventh and eighth grade students for many years. She began writing to provide struggling students novels that were age appropriate but easy to read.

Sara is a graduate of Rutgers College in New Brunswick, New Jersey. She is a teacher at South Orange Middle School in South Orange, New Jersey. She is a member of the National Council of Teachers of English, the Society of Children's Book Writers and Illustrators, and the New Jersey Education Association.

Sara currently resides in Whitehouse Station, New Jersey with her husband, Jamie, and their son, Benjamin.